STUMBLING UPON

Book Two—The Hamilton Harbor Legacy Series

If you like a sweet, humorous love story that warms the heart, you'll enjoy *Stumbling Upon Romance*.
—*USA Today* best-selling author, Susan May Warren

Readers are saying ...

This book took me back to the summer of my childhood when the world was filled with exuberance, discovery, and joy—a time when troubles were yet far away in the future.

... loved all the characters, especially the dogs.

With the references to reading devotions and keeping a journal, this story motivated me to start journaling again.

Stumbling Upon Romance provides an escape into the lives of people living at a gentler pace in a gentler place.

... loved the story, characters, and being a major animal lover, I enjoyed reading about the different dogs.

I could relate to clumsy Claudia who felt she had a black cloud hanging over her and disasters that followed her about. Like the heroine, I had to learn to roll with whatever happened and look for the humor.

My imagination was led captive in Hamilton Harbor.

I enjoyed the hero in the story—strong, silent, heart of gold and good with Clover (the dog).

The author drew me into a place where I would abandon all earthly possessions to live!

STUMBLING UPON

Book Two—The Hamilton Harbor Legacy Series

SALLY JO PITTS

PUBLISHING THE POSITIVE

ELK LAKE PUBLISHING INC
Plymouth, Massachusetts

Cover and Interior Design: Derinda Babcock

Editor(s): Cristel Phelps, Deb Haggerty

Author Represented by the Seymour Agency

PUBLISHED BY: Elk Lake Publishing, Inc., 35 Dogwood Drive, Plymouth, MA 02360, 2019

Library Cataloging Data

Names: Pitts, Sally Jo (Sally Jo Pitts)

Stumbling Upon Romance: Book Two—The Hamilton Harbor Legacy Series / Sally Jo Pitts

202 p. 23cm × 15cm (9in × 6 in.)

Description: Accident-prone dog groomer, Claudia Stewart, is a newcomer to Hamilton Harbor, Florida. She hopes to shed her black cloud image, fit in the community, and find a guy who will knock her off her feet. Instead, Claudia and her giant schnauzer client knock handyman Pete Cullen off his feet and leave him hanging from an overhead beam.

Identifiers: ISBN-13: 978-1-951080-50-1 (trade) | 978-1-951080-51-8 (POD) | 978-1-951080-52-5 (e-book)

Keywords: contemporary romance, inspirational, beach read, South, small town romance, women's fiction, mystery

LCCN: 2019951957 Fiction

Acknowledgments

No book is completed without many dedicated helpers to make it happen. This list is hardly exhaustive, but I gratefully acknowledge the following:

Editors Deb Haggerty and Cristel Phelps, Elk Lake Publishing, Inc.

Julie Gwinn, The Seymour Agency.

Marcia Lahti—for untold hours of reading, encouragement, comments and suggestions on the many versions of this manuscript

Susie May Warren, Rachel Hauck and the team at My Book Therapy for their advice, direction, and support.

Beta readers who reviewed the manuscript before publication.

My husband, LaVelle, who went to reside with the Lord before this book made it into print. He was always there for me with encouragement and support over the several years this story was written and rewritten. He above all would agree with the sentiment the book portrays—that God has a purpose for us all and loves us just as we are.

For we are his workmanship, created in Christ Jesus for good works, which God prepared beforehand, that we should walk in them.
—(Ephesians 2:10 ESV)

1 The Flower Co. Hdqtr.
2 Old Whart/Edgar Feldman home
3 Thomas Feldman Hous
4 Edgar Feldman House
5 Gardner Feldman House
6 House/Feldman Hunt/Garden Club
7 The Mayoral Park
8 Harbor Town "Royal" Bistro
9 Southern Life Rally
10 The Governor's Club
11 The Top of the Harbor Apartments
12 Library
13 City Hall
14 Hamilton Harbor Marina

Chapter 1

Would she ever escape misfortune?

Florida's early morning sun bore down on Claudia Stewart, who was stuck outside her dog grooming shop in downtown Hamilton Harbor.

"Good grief. Now my apron's caught in the door." Harvey, her giant schnauzer client, sat down—again—on the sidewalk in front of The Pampered Pooch and cocked his furry head.

"At this rate, we'll never make it to Elaine's."

Shoving Harvey's leash between her knees, she jiggled the key into the old-fashioned keyhole and opened the door, freeing her grooming apron. The business sign, with clock hands set at 9:00 and 5:00, clunked against the door glass, accenting her pride in being a new business owner.

Claudia closed the door behind her a third time. She'd already returned to retrieve her purse. The sun's rays foreshadowed another hot, humid summer day in the northwest Florida coastal town, and the warm air intensified the scent of vanilla bean coat conditioner on Harvey *and* her.

"Harvey," Claudia sniffed her shirt, "I smell like a well-groomed canine." The big, black dog, sporting a new haircut and bandana, perked up his ears and waggled his stump of a tail.

She squinted to read the time on her wristwatch. "Seven o'clock. Should be plenty of time to walk you, and ..." Claudia snapped her fingers. "Before we set out this time, I'd better make sure I have the horseshoe for Elaine's grand opening."

Harvey blinked at her with black, shiny eyes underneath neatly trimmed brow fringe and sat back down. Claudia stepped on his leash, freeing her hands to check her purse. She felt the hard, cold metal and held it up for Harvey to see. "Let's hope this horseshoe brings Elaine good luck with her bistro."

But Harvey's focus had gone elsewhere. Pointy ears stood soldier erect, his front shoulders twitched. Claudia turned. The piercing gold eyes of a sleek black cat stared back.

"Harr-veey," Claudia cautioned.

The cat sprinted.

The big dog lunged, yanking the leash from under Claudia's foot. His leap sent the horseshoe clattering down the sidewalk and her flip-flop soaring.

"Harvey!" Claudia's cry did nothing to slow Harvey's chase. "You expect me to catch you wearing flip-flops and carrying a purse?" She retrieved her shoe and ran—the rubber soles flapping against her heels.

The cat raced down the sidewalk. Harvey woofed in clumsy pursuit, while Claudia dashed after her runaway. Old brick store fronts, green-striped awnings sheltering rejuvenated stores, and crepe myrtles lining Main Street blurred. Seagulls from the harbor at the end of the street circled and squawked. Deep-sea fishing boats she would never dare step foot on bucked in the choppy waters. Past the "Opening Soon" sign at Elaine's Harbor Town Bagel Bistro, Claudia followed the raucous barks.

"Harvey, stop!"

Harvey let out a high-pitched yip as he ran into the breezeway beside the bistro.

Claudia rounded the corner. A tall stepladder rattled past her, smashed against the corridor's stucco wall, and crashed on its side. Harvey's leash wrapped tightly around the ladder base, stopping him just short of the cat. The dog panted, his long tongue dripping wet droplets onto the concrete walkway.

The cat hissed.

Could her morning get any worse?

She heard the ominous sound of glass scraping against stucco and turned just in time to catch a fluorescent light bulb before it hit the pavement.

She'd missed her morning run, but her heart was still getting a workout.

Righting the light bulb against the wall, the sound of a throat clearing made her jump and look up. Dangling above her head were two booted feet. A man, arms stretched taut, clung to an overhead beam. A light fixture swung precariously at his side.

The whole episode took seconds to unfold but would have taken hours to choreograph.

"This is awful." Claudia wrung her hands.

"How about moving my ladder back."

"Oh, of course." Spinning around, Claudia hung her toe on the side of the ladder, and pain shot through every nerve of her foot.

"Yikes," she yelped. "Harvey, how in the world did you manage to get so tangled?"

The acidic taste of her morning coffee inched up the back of Claudia's throat, and her hands shook as she worked to free the leash.

"Hey," a woman stepped from the building next door, "let me help." She stooped down and lifted the ladder for Claudia to free the leash.

"You are a Godsend," Claudia said, breathless.

The dog grumbled.

The cat crouched and sent a hostile look at Harvey.

Claudia gave the dog a quick side tug with the leash. "Harvey, you stay put."

"Ladies—the ladder?"

"Sorry." Claudia winced, got a firm grip on Harvey's leash, and helped her rescuer reposition the ladder.

"Here you go, Pete," the woman said to the guy overhead.

The rubber soles of the man's work boots squeaked a sigh of relief against the metal ladder as he regained firm footing.

"I'm Kali Reppen," the woman said holding out her hand to Claudia. "I work for Southern Life Realty." She nodded toward the business next door.

"Claudia Stewart. Thanks so much for the help."

Kali had a confident grip, precision-cut, shoulder-length blonde hair with bright highlights, sparkly white teeth suitable for a tooth-whitening commercial, and stylish high-heeled shoes—probably a size six.

"I'm a friend of Elaine's, the one who is opening the bistro." Claudia pointed to the door across the breezeway from the realty office.

"I, for one, will be glad when she's officially open. Fresh bagel and brewed coffee smells coming out of the bistro have been torturing me for days." Kali closed her eyes to sniff the aromas escaping the café.

"I, for another one, could use some help up here."

"Sorry, Pete." Kali directed her comments upward. "These smells keep me mesmerized." To Claudia she said, "That guy up there, whose feet you knocked out from under him, is Pete Cullen."

Pete peered down at her. She'd rather have met him eye-to-eye with a nice handshake. With him towering high above her, Claudia felt like a little kid called to the principal's office for misbehavior. "I'm so sorry for this disaster."

"I'm just glad to get my feet back on something solid. Do you see a couple of bolts down there?"

"Hold on." Kali said.

"I've been doing that," Pete muttered.

Claudia looked up. He had a light fixture propped on his shoulder.

"I'll help." Desperate to salvage the situation, Claudia tied Harvey to the wrought iron railing near the pet watering fountain Elaine had installed and set her purse in a chair beside him.

With Harvey secured, the black cat emerged.

The feline raised her whiskered face and, as if sufficiently satisfied with the upheaval she'd created, gave a regal farewell wave with her tail and trotted down the corridor to the alley behind.

Harvey protested with a low growl. "Harvey," Claudia used her pointed index finger, "shush."

The dog tilted his head to one side. Claudia lowered her finger in defeat. "Gotta' love ya'." She shrugged and patted his big head. Harvey responded with a sloppy, wet lick on her arm.

"Good heavens," She wiped her arm with the bottom of her apron and joined Kali to search on hands and knees for the bolts.

"Found one." Kali climbed a few steps up the ladder. "Here you go, Pete."

"Maybe you should have asked for hazard pay with this job," Kali told Pete, flashing a teasing smile Claudia's way.

"You run The Pampered Pooch down the street." Kali made the remark more as a statement of fact than a question.

"Yes. How did you know?"

Kali nodded toward Harvey and Claudia's apron printed with romping puppies. "Good guess?"

"Oh." Claudia laughed. "You are a good guesser. I opened for business last month." Claudia knelt and began sweeping her hands over the pavement. "This is so embarrassing. Not the way I wanted to meet people."

In Atlanta, the incident wouldn't have mattered much—just another oddity in a sea of many. But life had brought her to this small Florida

Panhandle town where anonymity wouldn't be so easy. She only had one chance to make a good first impression. Creating havoc wasn't what she had in mind.

"Oh, I don't know," Kali said. "I think you've come up with a novel way to get introduced. Where are you from?"

Easy to answer for most, but not Claudia. She'd lived several places since she lost her parents at age nine. "Long story, but most recently Atlanta."

"Wow. I'd love to move to a big city like Atlanta if I had the right job opportunity."

"The city can offer opportunity if you're willing to sacrifice the small-town community you have here. I used to have an hour-long commute to work. Now I'm just seconds away. Moving here has been a blessing."

Claudia's knee crunched against something hard. "Ouch."

"Your knee found the bolt?" Kali asked.

Claudia smiled, grasped the bolt, and swept her hand high in the air as if displaying a winning trophy. "Teamwork."

But triumph was short-lived when the bolt took flight. Claudia watched in disbelief as the hard projectile zeroed in, like a programmed missile, on the fluorescent bulb she had just saved.

"Nooooo." Claudia moaned the word in hopes of undoing the inevitable.

The bolt evaded Kali's grab attempt and hit its target. The bulb exploded and crashed to the pavement. Shattered bits of glass and powder lay scattered along the corridor walkway.

Pete let out a grunt.

Claudia covered her mouth with her hands. Disaster, her hallmark, reared its head. Would these broken bits of glass shatter her new beginning? Fresh starts were supposed to go well, but for Claudia, not so much.

Pete watched from his overhead perch. The nerves in his arms still tingled after hanging from the beam. His shoulder carried the weight of the light fixture while the bedlam from the broken light bulb played out.

"What's going on out here?" Elaine Robinson poked her head with its pixie haircut out of the bistro entrance. Flour dotted her face and apron.

"Come on out, you're missing all the action," Kali said.

Claudia groaned.

Pete's eyes strayed from the shattered bulb to the girl with the fiery red hair below. Her gestures, explaining the fiasco to Elaine, sparked his interest. The kind of spark he made a vow to extinguish like a bucket of water on hot embers if the urge ever came up again.

Kali diverted his attention. "Here's the other bolt."

"Tell Elaine that powder is an environmental hazard. It needs to be bagged up properly."

"She knows," Kali said. "Elaine explained the same thing to me. Claudia's bringing another bulb."

"Think she can handle it?" Pete said.

"Sure. Just a bad break." She sent Pete a wink. "No pun intended."

Pete squinted his eyes at Kali. "Cute."

Claudia returned, grasping in both hands a fluorescent bulb protected by its cardboard cover. Kali's cell phone buzzed, and she checked the caller ID. "I'd better take this in the office. Good meeting you, Claudia. I guess I'll be seeing you around."

Claudia nodded. "Thanks for your help."

Pete secured the fixture with the bolts as Kali went back in her office. Little wonder Kali wound up in sales after high school. It was a lucrative way to use her knack for maneuvering whatever—and whomever—she wanted to suit her whims.

"I'm not leaving this to chance. I'm handing the bulb to you in the package," Claudia said.

The look of determination on her face pricked Pete's heart, surprising him. He gave her a heavy nod. Her expression softened, then brightened, as she successfully transferred the bulb to him.

"Did it!" She let out a huge breath, as if she'd achieved a huge milestone.

"Thanks." Pete tested the fixture with a tug to make sure it was secure and added the fluorescent bulb.

Elaine returned with heavy cardboard, duct tape, and a plastic bag for clean-up.

"Elaine, would you flip the switch inside the door?" Pete called down.

"I'll do it." Claudia said. She stepped toward the door and collided with Elaine. The duct tape went flying and landed right in front of Harvey. He clamped it in his teeth, as if holding a fat Frisbee.

Claudia scurried to retrieve the tape. "Good boy."

Harvey responded by wagging his rear end, making the wrought iron chairs clang together.

Pete shook his head.

She handed Elaine the tape and grabbed the bistro doorknob. "Which switch do you want turned on?"

"Far right."

The light flickered and came to its full brightness, illuminating the corridor.

"Yay!" Claudia clapped her hands.

Harvey barked.

Elaine looked at Pete. "Jeff will be proud of the increased lighting in the breezeway."

Pete thought that installing the fixture could be like training for her husband's SWAT team but opted to say, "You need good lighting for security." He climbed down the ladder, thankful to reach solid ground.

"I wanted the two of you to meet. I guess you have now." Elaine said.

"Indeed, I guess we have."

Claudia winced. "Sorry for the crash meeting."

She had amazing green eyes.

"It's all over now."

She bit at her lower lip and turned to finish helping Elaine with the cleanup.

Pete folded and leaned his ladder against the wall. What an inane remark—it's all over now. Couldn't he have come up with something better than that?

"Why don't you two come in," Elaine said. "I have a new recipe I want you to test. Pete, I set aside *This Old House* magazines that were donated to the lending library for you."

"I'll help." Claudia said. She grabbed her purse, told Harvey to "hang in there," then tripped over the threshold while entering the bistro.

Elaine might be wise to turn down assistance from this girl.

Inside, the tantalizing smell of baking dough flavored the air. Today's experiment carried a spicy scent. His role as a tester had been a fringe

9

benefit while he worked getting the bistro ready to open. After washing up, he picked up a *This Old House* magazine and settled into a pub chair at one of the bistro tables.

Claudia emerged from the kitchen drying her hands. "I'm really sorry about knocking you off your ladder. That wasn't a very good way to introduce myself." A sincere smile lit up her eyes.

To divert his gaze, Pete did all he knew to do. He looked down and said, "No problem."

Uneasiness took over. Why couldn't he just relax? He could handle listening better than holding a conversation. Opening his mouth meant running the risk of saying the wrong thing.

He tried to focus on the table of contents in the magazine but still heard Elaine talking to Claudia.

"How do you like the shelves Pete built for the lending library you suggested?"

"They're perfect."

"I distributed flyers to merchants on Main Street asking for library donations. The response has been wonderful."

"I'm afraid the library idea was a little self-serving. I've been able to whittle down the overgrown book collection that threatens to take over my little apartment."

"Self-serving or not, having books and magazines available for customers is a great idea. Right, Pete?"

Pete grunted his reply and tried to study the magazine in front of him.

Elaine headed back to the kitchen. "The new bagel samples are coming up."

Nothing on the page in front of him registered. He was aware only of the sweet scent of vanilla as Claudia approached his table. She lifted one of the magazines, and when she opened the cover, a bookmark fluttered to the floor.

Picking up the marker, she read out loud, "Love your neighbor as yourself." She handed the item to Pete. "That's a good idea, don't you think?"

Pete fingered the bookmark made of blue construction paper with neat black calligraphy print. "Depends on what you think of yourself," he said and handed the bookmark back to her. He tried to concentrate on a table-refinishing article, but few words penetrated. Silence emanated from Claudia—the kind that anticipates chitchat. Not his strong suit.

Elaine came out of the kitchen bringing blessed, aromatic relief to his discomfort.

"Try these." She placed a plate of bite-size bagel samples on the table. "These treats are my version of the Czech Klobasnek. That's sausage wrapped in bread dough."

The word Czech evoked a memory of Pete's one-time serious relationship. A memory that left him resolved to stay away from any romantic attachments. He sampled the fresh bagel spiced with a juicy hot dog center.

"Klo-bas-what?" Claudia asked. "I call them pigs in a blanket." She bit into one, gave a moan of delight, and gestured with her hands. "You've got a winner here. Call them whatever you like."

Pete agreed. "They'll be a big hit."

"Thanks, guinea pigs. How about something to drink?"

"A latté for me."

"Coffee, black, please."

"Plain black?" Claudia said. "How uninteresting."

She made the remark with a hint of laughter that put a chink in Pete's armor. He raised one eyebrow and said, "Suits me." He meant his return as a flat comment.

She responded with an anxious, "Just kidding," and turned away to help Elaine.

Had he come across too hard? He didn't mean to. But that was his manner, and short responses did serve to … to what? Give him a safe wall to hide behind? Probably.

Claudia returned with coffees in hand. "Here you go, sir." She presented his coffee as if the drink was an award. "No frills, no extras, just the pure, unadulterated java."

Coffee sloshed out as she set the cup down.

"Oops." She dabbed at the spill. "I always bring extra napkins."

Pete looked up and puzzled over the clumsy girl who seemed determined to engage him. With a nod, he accepted the coffee and attempted to return to his article.

Claudia picked up the bookmark. "Since we tend to look out for our own interests, maybe we should do the same thing for others?"

She made the comment as if they'd been discussing the meaning. He should make some response. "Suppose so," was all his reserve allowed but was enough for Claudia to take a seat at the table.

Pete needed a place to focus his eyes and reached for the bookmark. He knew the Scripture, had heard the sentiment taught in Sunday school and preached in the pulpit. But the verse had always confused him and seemed self-centered—the notion of loving yourself. And what if you were unlovable? What then? Was it even possible to love your neighbor?

Pete took a deep breath and pushed the bookmark back in Claudia's direction. He sipped his coffee and wished the warmth could soothe his edginess. Oh, to relax and enjoy a good brewed cup of coffee—not like the strong stuff served when he worked on the oil rigs. But that desire was proving hard in the presence of this bright-eyed girl with the curly hair.

"Do you suppose black cats come into our lives to push us into thinking of someone other than ourselves?" Claudia asked.

Her question blindsided him. "Black cats?"

"Like the one Harvey chased. Instead of being bad luck, what if they were meant to keep us from dwelling on ourselves?"

"So you could concentrate on the poor guy that was about to make a twenty-foot drop?"

"Yeah, like that."

He stared at her a second. Cute as a puppy. Her sage-green eyes complimented her coppery-red hair and fair skin sprinkled with freckles. He shook his head and managed a sip of coffee. "I always heard black cats brought either good or bad luck. Not that I believe in that sort of thing."

"Luck." She slammed her coffee down, spilling some. "The horseshoe."

Elaine was busy polishing the glass on the display case.

"Elaine, I dropped the horseshoe I was bringing you for good luck."

Elaine twirled her cleaning rag and smiled. "I don't want to miss out on anything good sent my way."

Claudia picked up a napkin from her stockpile and wiped up the spilled coffee.

"Watch my coffee and keep an eye on Harvey." Claudia spoke to Pete as if they were a twosome, then rushed out the door.

Baffled, Pete stared after her. He glanced out the bistro window and saw that Harvey was snoozing in the shade of a green-striped table umbrella. What had he done to warrant Claudia's interest? He'd tried not to encourage her, yet she seemed bent on including him. And something deep inside him—he hated to admit—kind of liked the attention.

Chapter 2

If trouble came in threes, maybe she was done for the day.

Claudia retraced the frenzied route she'd taken chasing Harvey. The ladder, light bulb, and duct tape incidents could happen to anyone. Right? But why her?

The sun peered over the buildings that lined Main Street now waking up. Car activity had picked up, and an "open" sign hung in the antique shop window across the street. At the end of the street, a few joggers ran along the marina. Claudia enjoyed running when the objective wasn't a wayward dog.

Light breeze from the bay struggled to stir the humid air. She used the corner of her apron to wipe at the perspiration dampening her forehead and hair. *Did she still have a black cloud over her head?* Even under a cloudless sky on this hot July morning, the weight of troublesome baggage clung to her. She was almost back at her shop when a ray of sunlight broke through the alley and spotlighted gleaming metal underneath a bush.

"Hallelujah." Reenergized, Claudia wasted no time getting back to the bistro, where Harvey lay sprawled in the shade. She wiped at the moisture on her face with the back of her hand. "Gramma called days like these, dog days. How come, Harvey?"

An eyelid opened at half-mast to gaze at Claudia.

"So hot you just want to lie around like a dog, maybe?"

Harvey wiggled his rear.

"Looks like I'm on to something."

Gramma had sayings and opinions on a lot of things—like "You need to take ballet to make you more graceful."

That didn't work. Gramma had tried hard to reshape and refine her klutzy granddaughter. But her efforts didn't prevent Claudia from acquiring her "Black Cloud" nickname—or the most creative one—"Cloudia."

"Now's my chance for an image change. Right boy?"

Harvey twitched an ear one tick to the right.

"I'll get this horseshoe hung for Elaine, then we'll get back to The Pampered Pooch."

Both ears twitched a couple more millimeters.

Claudia gave Harvey a pat on the head. At the bistro's glass door, she paused to straighten a wayward curl she could see in her reflection. She took a deep breath and entered.

"Success!"

She felt like a victor home from a mission, but her return went unheralded. Elaine was out of sight, and Pete—absorbed in his reading—didn't even look up. Was he antisocial or just ignoring her? Claudia couldn't blame him. She couldn't fault any guy for avoiding her. Catastrophes followed her like a bug attracted to a light.

Elaine came out of the kitchen. "You found my good luck?"

"Sure did." Claudia plunked the heavy metal into Elaine's outstretched hand.

"What will this do for me?" Elaine asked examining the U-shaped iron as if it might have magical powers.

"My Gramma said a horseshoe brings good luck," Claudia lowered her voice, "but I think it's more for decoration. However, I must tell you, when I hung one in my shop, I got my first customer."

"I appreciate you thinking of me." Elaine said. "Pete, since you've got your ladder here, would you mind hanging the horseshoe for me?"

Pete raised his head just enough for his eyes to clear the top of the magazine. He rose from his chair, wordless, and headed out the door. Hopefully, to get the ladder.

"Claudia, you supervise. I need to finish in the kitchen. By the way, come to church supper and Bible study with me tonight. It's a good way to meet people, and you don't have to worry about fixing dinner."

"Sounds good." Claudia went to the door to hold it open for Pete. His body language said he was unenthusiastic but compliant.

"You didn't get to finish your coffee. I can hang it, if you don't mind me using your ladder."

"I'll handle hanging the horseshoe. You didn't get to finish your coffee, either." He spoke with a matter-of-fact tone but not unkind. "Where do you want it hung?"

"Right here, over the entrance."

Pete positioned the ladder at the front door and turned the bolt lock.

"I'd rather not end up hanging from the door frame if someone decides to come in."

He spoke to the room at large, but Claudia knew the comment was for her benefit. She studied Pete as he went to his toolbox beside the bookshelves. He stood over six-feet tall, had long, jean-clad legs topped with a blue T-shirt that accented broad shoulders. He wore his hair in a short bristly military cut that matched his curt remarks.

Her mind went back to his comment about the verse on the bookmark. "It depends on what you think of yourself." A profound statement. What did she think of herself? At this point in her life, mostly that she had a propensity for calamities and wanted that fact to change.

Pete came back with a hammer and a couple of nails. "Just give me instructions."

The sight of his intense blue eyes trained on her, made her voice squeak. "Okay."

He climbed the ladder, set the hammer and nails on the ladder shelf and held the horseshoe up, forming a rainbow over the door.

"Turn it the other way, like a U."

"Up or down matters?"

"Sure. My Gramma said the horseshoe holds your luck inside. All your luck would fall out the other way."

Pete sighed, positioned the horseshoe sides up, and hammered two nails on either side.

Claudia stepped back to examine the placement. "It's a little lop-sided. Can you lift the left side a little?"

"Hand me a nail puller from my toolbox."

What in the world was a nail puller? "Nail puller? I don't—"

"Flat head screwdriver will do."

"I know what that is."

Happy to get a chance for reprieve, Claudia opened his toolbox. Everything was neat and organized. She spotted the screwdriver and took the tool to him.

Prying the horseshoe loose, the screwdriver slipped and jabbed the back of his left hand.

"Oh no. Are you okay?"

"Yeah." Pete pulled out the nail and repositioned the horseshoe. "How's this?"

"Looks perfect to me," Elaine said, returning from the kitchen.

"Yes, just right." Claudia saw blood trickling down the back of Pete's hand. "Pete. You're bleeding. Let me doctor that for you. I've got antiseptic and a Band-Aid in my purse."

"You carry that sort of thing with you?" Pete asked as he stepped down from the ladder.

Claudia nodded her head. "I ... uh ... I like to be prepared." A practice she'd started out of necessity years ago.

She rummaged through her purse and located the zippered bag containing antiseptic wipes, a tube of antibiotic salve, and Band-Aids.

Pete seemed so self-reliant, she was a little surprised and pleased he held his hand out to her.

Claudia cleaned and applied ointment. "This will prevent infection." Their eyes made contact for the second time. The intensity had softened. Her heart made a weird skip while she opened the adhesive strip wrapper.

Elaine inspected Pete's wound. "I appreciate you hanging the horseshoe. I'm so sorry you got hurt."

"No big deal," he said to Elaine.

To Claudia, he said, "Thank you," as she applied the bandage. "I'll put this ladder on the truck and be back for my tools. I need to get to another job."

Claudia returned his hammer and screwdriver to his toolbox and the first aid kit to her purse. She cleared the table of their cups and was behind the counter when the clatter of tools hitting the floor jarred her. She whirled about and pressed her hand to her mouth. Pete stood holding the emptied toolbox by the handle.

"I'm so sorry. I guess I didn't close the latch right. Let me help."

"No," he said abruptly. Then softer, and measured, he said, "I'd rather put my tools away myself. I know where everything goes."

"At least, let me hand things to you."

"Really, it's okay. I can manage."

Manage better without her help. Unfortunately, he was right.

18

She had a date. But not the kind Claudia had hoped for with birthday number twenty-seven on its way. However, a church date with Elaine would have pleased her parents, especially if she found a church home.

Claudia pulled into Elaine's tree-lined Meadow Lake subdivision. Homes nestled around a park with a walking trail, small lake, and playground brought back memories of the little neighborhood where she lived before her parents died. Meadow Lake looked like a perfect place to settle down and raise a family—a place to call home. But for her, there was the little matter of finding a mate. Her mate might have to be a proverbial "knight in shining armor" to survive her accident proneness. Or could she change? New town, new business, new friends—maybe, just maybe—the new venue would bring the change she needed.

Pulling into Elaine's brick drive, she stepped out of her car and stretched the tense muscles in her neck. The comb-out of her last client, a feisty Maltese, had been a challenge.

Elaine greeted her at the door. "I appreciate you picking us up. When Jeff works late, he meets us at church. Your driving will keep us from ending up with two cars to take home."

"My pleasure. Living and working at the grooming shop, I don't get out much. What I want to know is how you found a good-looking, hard-working guy who also keeps a beautiful yard." With a sweep of her hand, she indicated the expanse of neatly trimmed landscape.

Elaine grinned. "Jeff was God-ordained. He keeps us safe and has yard work as a hobby. He says lawn care relaxes him." Only six years out of college, Elaine with her black hair in a short-cropped haircut could pass for a high schooler. She stepped her petite, five-foot frame aside and motioned for Claudia to enter. "Girls," she called out, "Miss Claudia is here."

Claudia made a point to step around the iron doorstop she'd tripped on the last time she visited. Four-year-old Cindy and five-year-old Mara greeted Claudia in the tiled front hall.

"Come here," Cindy said grabbing Claudia's hand. Mara led the way down the entry hall to the den. They proudly pointed to a large square cocktail table covered with papers and crayons.

"We're making posters for Mommy's restaurant."

"You must have inherited your mom's advertising skills." Claudia admired their hand-drawn signs on construction paper depicting bagels, cups of coffee, and the invitation to "Com to Momys Restrant."

"I couldn't have asked for better promoters." Elaine beamed. "Girls, you need to finish the sign you're working on, put away the supplies, and put your shoes on." To Claudia, she said, "Come in the kitchen, I'm making snacks for the children's program that's held while we're in Bible study."

"As if you didn't spend enough time in the kitchen today."

"It can be tiring, but I'm enjoying the challenge."

Claudia followed Elaine into her cozy kitchen. The counter and bar stools divided the work area from a breakfast nook. A bay window that overlooked the backyard framed a swing set and playhouse. "Did Jeff build the playhouse?"

"He and a couple of patrolman buddies designed and built the little house in one weekend. The girls love it." Elaine washed some apples and began coring them.

"I bet." Observing the curtained windows and red door took Claudia back to her own backyard as a child and the playhouse her dad had built for her. She hosted tea parties there for her dolls, but sometimes her parents would graciously squeeze into the tiny chairs and declare her lemonade the best ever. She'd felt happy, safe, and secure in her miniature house until the plug got pulled and her home, parents, and playhouse were sucked out of her life.

She took a deep breath. "Elaine, do you ever think about how our college foursome turned out—you, me, Emme, and Izzie?"

"What do you mean?"

"Emme reconnected with her first love and lives on a Southern plantation. Izzie's interior design business is taking off, making Emme extra busy at The Flower Cottage—I rarely see her, and her shop is right behind mine. You have a new business, wonderful husband, two beautiful girls, a nice home ..."

Elaine stopped her apple slicing and looked Claudia squarely in the eyes. "You'll find a special someone and have a home, too, one day. You'll see."

"I don't know." Claudia wilted onto one of the bar stools at the kitchen counter. "A dark cloud seems to trail me like the puff of dirt around Charlie Brown's buddy, Pigpen."

"There you go, dwelling on the negative."

"Well, you saw what happened. I knocked poor Pete off his ladder, he's wounded 'cause I had him move that horseshoe, then all his tools go crashing to the floor. Thanks, by the way, for not saying why I keep a first-aid kit in my purse."

"Your secret is safe with me," Elaine said, stuffing apple slices into snack bags.

"But won't be for long, I'm afraid. Chihuahuas are known to be nervous, pit bulls to be mean, and Claudia Stewart is an accident waiting to happen. Keeping a first-aid kit handy seems the most humane thing for me to do."

Elaine pressed her hands against the counter. "Look, silly labels put on you in the past need to stay in the past. We both swore not to mention them. The dog knocked Pete off that ladder, and Pete is the one who wounded his hand. Don't read anything more into the mishaps."

Elaine pulled carrots from the refrigerator, took them to the sink, and began peeling the skins.

"What about Jimmy? We were as good as engaged when I knocked over a stack of chairs that brought down the reception table at his sister's wedding. He left town."

"You have to leave town when you join the army."

"Yeah, well, I think he thought his life would be safer taking his chances getting shot at than sticking around me. He wasn't out of boot camp six weeks before he met someone and is getting married."

"How do you know the army and his marriage wasn't all part of God's plan to position him, and ultimately you, for the right person to come into your life?"

"If that's the case, where's my Mr. Right? I'm almost twenty-seven."

"Like your time is running out? I thought you turned twenty-six a couple of months ago."

"I did, so that means I'm going on twenty-seven."

"Now you're getting melodramatic, my friend." Elaine began slicing the carrots.

"I'm prattling. Can I help you?"

"No thanks."

"Best to avoid cut fingers?"

Elaine cocked and shook her head. "No. No need to dirty another knife. Be careful about adding your negative take on what I say."

Claudia slipped from the stool and looked out the window at the little house. Calamity Claudia was one of the first labels kids had given her. "I know you're right, but the fact is calamities still happen when I'm around.

I wonder why I can't shed them. Remember in college when I threw up on my blind date's shoes? He never asked me out again, and he was cute for a blind date."

"The sun was merciless at the football game, with humidity to match. Others felt queasy that day."

"Yeah, but nobody threw up on their date. Then there's Aunt Lucy, who took me in and tripped on my mega-feet, broke her hip, and ended up in rehab. I think I have a bad luck gene."

"Would you stop? Think of the positives. You've always admitted going into the children's home when your aunt broke her hip was good for you, and today, you met two nice people. So what if the way you met them was … unique?"

"A unique curiosity." Claudia dropped her gaze to the countertop and traced the line in the granite with her finger. "If I could only change, you know, fit in. Maybe *then* I'd find my niche and my Prince Charming."

"You are well on your way to finding your niche with your dog grooming business. Dogs adore you."

Claudia scrunched her face into a pout. "Dogs love everybody."

"Not like you." Elaine traded light-hearted for serious. "Look. You've acquired a ready-made business in a town on the verge of a reawakening. Talk to Pete about the improvements you want to make, and you'll certainly fit in with the Downtown Reconstruction Board plans. Just be you, and Prince Charming will show up when you're not looking. That's how it was for Jeff and me."

"I know. You ran into the back of his police car."

"See? Fall in love with someone who falls in love with your flaws and thinks you're perfect just the way you are. Clumsy isn't always bad."

Claudia rolled her eyes. "Don't be so smug."

"Listen. Mishaps happen to other people. You don't have an exclusive."

Attempting a smile, Claudia drew in and released a deep breath before continuing. "Do you really think I'll ever find a guy who's tough enough to hang with klutzy me?"

"Of course." Elaine plunked her knife and cutting board in the sink. "No negative-speak, remember?"

"Fresh start. Positive thinking. No self-blame." Claudia repeated by rote.

"That's the ticket." Elaine gathered the sliced apples and carrots and stuffed them in a small cooler.

Claudia stood. "I need to find the booth that sells those tickets."

Chapter 3

Pete swiped at the perspiration trailing down his face. His morning run put him back at his apartment at 5:00 a.m. But sweating off last night's church supper did little to rid him of seeing Claudia across the room or warding off Francine Waterman's questions, "Cute, isn't she? Have you met her?"

Electronic beeps sounded a tune as Pete tapped the code allowing keyless entry. His place consisted of a plain living room-kitchen, bedroom, and bath-utility room—all he needed. Working on the oil rigs had taught him to be satisfied with essentials.

The preset coffeemaker wheezed itself awake. He showered, emerged refreshed, poured a cup of coffee, and settled on a stool at the counter that doubled as his desk. Pete looked forward to his morning Bible devotion. Normally, time with the Lord put his problems, ideas, and thoughts in perspective. But the words were just letters on the page this morning. A green-eyed redhead with wild curls invaded the white spaces.

He tried reading a verse aloud, "Delight yourself in the LORD and he will give you the desires of your heart." Pete had discovered the church Helping Hands Ministry was a good way to delight in the Lord. Helping someone in need made his day. And if dealing with the opposite sex was an issue, he felt safe working with women who were over seventy—sort of.

When Francine, a senior he did household repairs for, caught him watching Claudia at church, she made him feel like a kid caught sneaking a look at a student's test paper. Not only that, but Francine's eyes had glinted with matchmaking. Why were little old ladies compelled to see that single men or women didn't remain that way?

He willed his mind, infringed on by a vision of Claudia, to move on with his devotion. He reread the verse, which held special meaning for him today. To own the 1912 Hamilton house had always been the desire of his heart. The two o'clock meeting Kali had scheduled with the Hamilton sisters would put him a step closer.

He reached for the picture of the two and a half story American Farmhouse-style home attached to the bulletin board beside the counter. As a teenager, Pete fantasized about raising a family in the house. But foreign-born Lidia, who left him with a bruised heart, cured him of that dream. He no longer had need for a family-sized house but still looked forward to the restoration of the multi-bedroom home with separate garage apartment.

He fingered the photo that depicted well-groomed hedges and gardens, now overgrown and unkempt. The once straight and solid front steps and porch now sagged. Repairing the front steps and drooping porch would be his first project. A specific goal gave him a sense of direction—a good feeling.

Finishing his devotion time in prayer, Pete expressed thanks for his father who had taught him basic building skills. And because of the work ethic his father engrained in him as a youngster, he needed to get to Elaine's bistro. He had promised to paint the final coat of polyurethane on the bookshelves first thing this morning.

With the thought of the bistro, the image of Claudia tending his wound flashed in front of him. Like an annoying computer pop-up ad, there she was—the dog groomer with the Irish-setter red hair. Why did thoughts of her keep dogging him?

Claudia grabbed for Pete but couldn't quite reach him. Her brain, fuzzy, gradually cleared. She sat up, then flopped her head back against the pillow. A dream.

Pete must have been in her thoughts, since she'd seen him from a distance at church last night. She bear-hugged her pillow and allowed her mind to drift to his strong features and hard-to-read demeanor. With her eyes closed tight, she could see his penetrating, deep blue eyes.

Buzzzz.

The alarm startled her. Claudia pushed the alarm button to *off.*

This same alarm clock had awakened her in elementary school. No longer did she get the ten-minute follow-up from her mom or dad to make sure she didn't go back to sleep. Claudia stared at the red LED number that slipped from 5:00 to 5:01. The clock had also awakened her the day Gramma appeared in her room—lips pressed in a tight, thin line—to tell her she would never see her mom or dad again. If only she hadn't …

Claudia flung back her covers to throw off the "if onlys." If only her mom and dad hadn't gone on that cruise. If only Claudia hadn't broken her ankle. If only her parents hadn't rented a small craft to get back to her. If only there had been no storm, no damaged hull, no ocean currents that came out of the deep to suck their life out like quicksand.

Run.

As a part of her morning routine, running helped overcome pessimistic thoughts.

In the dim early morning light, her upstairs apartment with its high black ceiling took on cave-like qualities. Not the warm and cozy feel she'd envisioned for a home, but maybe that vision was for another day. She swung her feet over the edge of the bed and stepped onto the wood floor, cool and invigorating. She wanted to get an early start in order to help Elaine before opening her grooming shop.

In a matter of minutes, Claudia, dressed in running shorts and a tank top, was ready for her run. Her treadmill stood alongside the fourteen-foot arched window expanse that fronted Main Street.

She pulled back the wooden window covering fitted with rollers to reveal the panorama of streetlamps, brick-lined sidewalks, and tops of the crepe myrtles with bright white blossoms. The program selector on the treadmill beeped as she searched for a challenging program and pressed "start."

She enjoyed the morning view from her apartment but looked forward to running outside when she could find a running buddy. Running was one thing she discovered she could handle without major mishaps. But running also put her in an activity that required interaction, and … well … grade school classmates learned to steer clear. She'd been humiliated many a time by being picked last for a team. That's when the Calamity Claudia label first cropped up.

Taking long strides on the treadmill brought Claudia's mind to Pete and his long legs dangling over her head yesterday. She imagined herself running with Pete—the pace would be steady with no chitchat. The idea brought a smile to her face, but for now staying inside would be the safe thing to do.

Safe. Would she ever feel completely safe again? Having parents snatched from her so suddenly left her off balance. Living with Gramma, Aunt Lucy, and later the children's home gave her some sense of security but never like the surety of a home with her parents.

She finished her run, read her devotional, showered, and dressed. The wooden steps creaked their good morning as she trotted downstairs to the grooming shop. The daily newspaper lay on the floor by the front door mail slot. One of her perks—mail and newspaper delivery came right inside the shop. She grabbed the paper and greeted the little leprechaun statue on her appointment table—a gift from her grandmother.

"Mornin', O'Flannery," She gave him a cheery salute and romped back up the stairs, taking two at a time. The sun's rays now reached into her apartment to brighten and dispel the darkness of early morning.

She glanced at the headlines: *Property Line Dispute Divides Community. Car Bombing Kills Three in Israel. New Trial Denied.* The news was doing nothing to boost her commitment to think positive.

She flipped to the comic page. Her little finger caught the lid of her sugar bowl, sent the top flying across the table where it glanced off the chair, then fell to the floor and broke. Try as she might, her persistent cloud lingered.

She knelt to pick up the ceramic pieces of the broken lid. Would she really be able to start over here? She liked Elaine's suggestion to enlist Pete's help to put a fresh look into her shop. But he was standoffish. Should she risk asking him for remodeling help? He might turn the project down, but if she was to ever make a change, she needed to take a chance.

Pete pulled into the alley behind the bistro as Elaine was getting out of her car. He parked his truck and got out.

"Can I give you a hand?"

"Good timing." Elaine handed Pete a couple of bags and hurried to open the bistro back door. "If I'd arrived at six, like I planned, I wouldn't have to rush." A bit out of breath, Elaine unlocked the door.

Daylight was encroaching on the dark gray early morning sky, and seagulls squawked greetings overhead. Pete checked his watch.

"A quarter after six and it's shaping up to be another hot day. The weather forecast on the radio said we're in for temperatures in the high 90s with humidity to match. It's a good thing you're offering iced coffees along with the hot."

Pete set his load in the kitchen, returned to Elaine's SUV and helped her unload the rest.

"I've got to adjust my morning routine," Elaine plunked her bags on the work island in the middle of the kitchen. "I'm thankful Jeff's mom volunteered to keep the girls for the next few days until I get the bistro open for business. Jeff is babysitting this morning until his mom arrives."

"You are blessed to have the support of your family, but what about help here at the restaurant?"

"I've got a girl from church who starts tomorrow."

Elaine pushed through the kitchen door to the front counter and restaurant seating. Pete followed. The one small task light she'd left on illuminated the room with a soft glow like an early 1900s bronze photo.

Elaine took in a deep breath, and her exhale turned to a smile. "Witness a room filled with hopes and dreams. You helped me change the interior from a dusty 1950s makeover to the rich look of old brick and deep polished mahogany." She made a 360° turnaround. "Thanks for your patience and help in the bistro's transformation."

"My privilege. Refinishing all the wood taught me a lot."

"Glad to provide the means for you to develop your skills." She flashed a grin and turned on the overhead lights. "I guess you'll have lots of wood to refinish after you finalize the Hamilton house deal."

Pete nodded. "Like your vision for the bistro, my dream has always been to buy that place and fix it up." He ran his hand over the smooth surface of one of the library shelves. "But if the Hamilton sisters don't like my work, they won't sell me the house."

Elaine picked up a bib apron from the stack behind the customer counter and slipped it over her head. "Not a chance."

"Not everyone thinks as highly of me and my work as you."

Elaine stopped her apron tying. "Can I tell you something?"

"I guess." Pete averted eye contact and looked at the shelving.

"I've noticed you tend to sell yourself short. You don't believe in yourself, and you should."

Pete shrugged. The tips of his fingers followed the grain of the wood like a trail leading to nowhere. His former fiancée, if he could call her that, laughed and branded him a fool before she walked out. "Let's just say it's hard for me to do." He cleared his throat. "But that won't stop me from finishing your shelves."

"Well, anyhow, since the Hamilton house is just off Main Street, the restoration will be a plus for downtown improvement efforts. I hope you don't mind, but I suggested Claudia check with you on some facelifts for her shop."

She dropped that tidbit before walking back toward the kitchen. "I'm practicing bagel prep times today. Can I count on you for taste testing?"

"Always."

Work for Claudia? Pete ran his fingers over the curved, routed edges of the shelves that were in need of a light sanding before he applied the final finish coating. Working with wood gave him a sense of accomplishment. Too bad his confidence didn't transfer to personal relationships. Could he work with Claudia? With wood, he could plan and predict the results. He had his doubts about predictable outcomes with her.

Checking his supplies, Pete opened a partially used can of polyurethane. If there wasn't enough to finish the job, he had another can. He set to work sanding the shelving. In a moment, he heard rapping at the door and saw Claudia's trademark red hair through the glass. He stepped down from the ladder to let her in.

"Good morning."

Claudia's voice lightened his spirit. She wore her hair pulled into a ponytail, letting wisps of curls frame her face. Dressed in jeans and a T-shirt printed with *Dogs Leave Paw Prints Forever on Our Hearts,* she looked fresh and cheerful.

Pete acknowledged her entry with a nod. Elaine pushed through the kitchen door and greeted Claudia.

Resuming his sanding, Pete couldn't help hearing Elaine and Claudia talk.

"Elaine, I'm at your service."

"You are?"

"Yup. I have a two o'clock appointment with a poodle. My shop window clock reads, 'back at noon,' so I'm yours for the morning."

"You didn't have to close your shop, but honestly, I could use the help."

"Well, I hope I am of help. I managed to break the top of my sugar bowl just reading the newspaper this morning."

"How in the world?"

"My black cloud, hovering."

Pete saw Claudia draw an invisible circle over her head with her index finger.

Elaine gave Claudia a "what am I to do with you" look. "Your black cloud. There you go, owning it again."

Pete stepped from the ladder to retrieve a cleaning cloth and trash bag. Claudia grimaced and dipped her head down, accepting her scolding from Elaine. Black cloud? Hovering? What was that all about?

Giving Claudia a quick side hug, Elaine said, "Since you're here. Would you straighten my supplies behind the customer counter? You're a good organizer. I need to check on a batch of whole grain apple bagels I want you and Pete to sample."

A light and a beep from the coffee brewer signaled the coffee was ready. "You two help yourselves."

"Thanks. I'll drink a cup shortly," Pete said. He climbed the ladder again and wiped sanding residue into the bag.

"I saw you at church last night," Claudia said.

"You did?"

"You were busy talking to some ladies. I understand you do fix-it work for them."

Pete looked down just as Claudia walked toward the shelving. He uttered, "Look out," but not in time to prevent the tip of Claudia's shoe from knocking over the open can of polyurethane.

"Oh, no." The contents oozed out—the puddle spreading. "Elaine's new floor. What do we do?"

Pete scrambled down the ladder and set the can upright to prevent more spillage. He pressed his lips together and appraised the mess.

Claudia's forehead wrinkled, eyes pleading. "Should I get paper towels?"

"Ask Elaine for a large sponge."

Claudia rushed to the kitchen. Elaine came out, sponge in hand.

"Please let me help." Claudia said.

"I've got it." He grabbed the sponge and began working the spill evenly over the floorboards. Did his words come across with an irritated edge he didn't intend? The girl tried so hard to make up for mishaps, maybe too hard.

"I can't believe it. Typical clumsy me."

"It'll be okay," Elaine said.

Pete saw the anguish in Claudia's eyes and felt compelled to ease her guilt.

"I can spread it out. This section will just have an extra coat of protection."

"See?" Elaine said. "No harm done. Besides I could use extra protection on that part of the floor. I want customers to put these shelves to good use." A timer sounded in the kitchen. "Looks good. I need to check the oven." Elaine hurried back to the kitchen.

"I'm sorry to put you to extra work," Claudia said.

"Really, it's okay." Pete tried to reassure her and kept working the coating into the floor, spreading it along a line of wood planks to make the extra sheen less noticeable. The clear coating brought out the reddish-brown highlights in the wood grain—the same vibrant color of Claudia's hair.

Claudia knelt beside him. Her presence touched him like the pull of a magnet.

"Can I bring you anything else?" She spoke in a small uncertain voice.

Had he come across so harshly that she was afraid to talk to him? "You could hand me the can of mineral spirits." He pointed to his supplies arranged on a paint cloth.

"Sure."

Claudia picked up the can, hesitated, and checked the cap. Her attempts to please, an endearing quality.

"Here you are." She set the can beside him. "Anything else?"

"No." Pete added, "Thank you."

"You're welcome."

Her response came in a tone that said she really appreciated his kinder tone. Since he usually worked alone, he wasn't accustomed to worrying over hurt feelings or proper decorum.

Claudia went behind the front counter and began work on the organization task.

Elaine emerged from the back. "I took a batch of bagels out to cool."

"What do you think about grouping all the cups beside the coffeemaker and arranging the rest of these supplies near the register?"

"Good idea. Let's try it."

Their chatter became white noise while Pete worked.

Pete finished wiping the shelves, opened the new can of polyurethane for the final coat and noticed the topic of conversation had shifted.

"See. All done, no hitches."

"Mission accomplished." Claudia put her hands on her hips, sending a container of stir sticks sliding down the counter. She covered her face with her hands.

Elaine grabbed the sticks before they tumbled to the floor. "Disaster diverted."

Claudia dropped her hands. "Maybe my helping wasn't such a great idea."

"Nonsense. You help me stay quick on my feet." She paused and held up an index finger. "Actually, a prizefighting Prince Charming might be just what you need."

"What are you talking about?"

"You know, prizefighters—quick on their feet—find a man with quick reflexes and you've got your Prince Charming."

"Oh, very funny."

"You're the one who said you were looking for someone with the right fortitude to stand under what you claim is your black cloud."

"You're making me sound self-centered again."

"Well? Have you ever considered that you get so uptight that you make yourself more susceptible to bad things happening?"

"So, I just need to relax?"

"Won't hurt to try." Elaine squeezed Claudia's shoulder.

Pete caught himself staring and started back to work on the shelves.

"Listen," Elaine said, "another thing you can do to help is group those donated books into categories—like cooking, decorating, murder mysteries—you know."

"Glad to." Claudia stepped from behind the counter and went over to the books and magazines stacked against the wall.

"Bagel samples coming up." Elaine said, and went back into the kitchen.

Claudia started sorting while Pete continued to apply polyurethane to the shelves.

"Here's a shelving unit that would be perfect in my shop. Do you know how to build storage cubes like these?" She held up a magazine cover for Pete to get a closer look.

How should he respond? He wanted to be free to start on the Hamilton house as soon as possible, but her eyes, her very presence, drew him in. Pete shrugged, "Probably."

A paper strip fell to the floor.

"Another bookmark." Claudia picked it up and read, "Teach me your way, O Lord, and I will walk in your truth. Psalm 86:11."

Pete focused on her as she read, her closeness a little intoxicating—or was it the polyurethane? She'd finished reading, and it took a second for the words to register. He reeled in his thoughts and simply said, "Wisdom Scriptures. Always good advice."

"I can certainly use good advice."

Elaine backed through the kitchen door with a tray of sweet-smelling bagels. A hint of apple and cinnamon competed with the strong paint odor. "They're cool and ready to sample."

Pete snapped the lid on the polyurethane and placed the brush in a jar with mineral spirits. "Your shelves will be dry and ready for books this evening or first thing in the morning."

"Great." Elaine set the bagels on a table.

Claudia's face brightened, highlighting the sprinkle of freckles across her cheeks and nose. "Since you're finished here, could you come to my shop and give me some shelving ideas?"

He'd taken time off from the oil rigs and gotten caught up on church volunteer work to devote time to the Hamilton house. Taking on a project with an accident-prone girl didn't seem wise. But for Elaine's sake, he could at least look. "I suppose so."

The bistro entry bell rang as Kali walked in the door.

"Elaine, you're merciless. Those bagel smells crept across the breezeway, slipped under the office door and beckoned me, 'Come,'" Kali demonstrated with wiggly fingers, "'eat my bagels and drink of my coffee.'" She turned her palms up. "It's like I'm drawn against my will. There should be a law against this sort of thing."

"Then I'll cover these and hide them in the back," Elaine said picking up the tray. "I'd hate to entice you against your will."

"Not necessary. I shall set aside my will for the good of bageldom." She spoke in commanding highfalutin' tones, her specialty. Lifting a sample from the tray, she held the bread up to the light, sniffed, and pressed a finger with a pink-polished nail on the bagel. "The texture is firm, the color a perfect golden brown, the smell—divine." Pinching off a morsel, she popped the piece into her mouth, chewed slowly, then gradually nodded her approval. "It's fabulous."

The girls, spellbound, gave a collective sigh of relief.

"Now, could I get a little coffee to accompany this wonderful creation?" Kali batted her lashes to no one in particular and hopped up on a stool. "Light on the sugar, heavy on the cream."

"I know how you like your coffee," Elaine said, and laughed at Kali's drama. "Claudia, help me with the coffees."

Pete wrinkled his brow, "All the theatrics and that's your big analysis—it's fabulous?"

She shrugged. "All that's necessary," she said and sampled another bite of bagel. Vintage Kali. Her personality captivated people, including him in times past. When Elaine and Claudia returned with the coffees, the four gathered at the table.

"Looks like your horseshoe brought a customer, Claudia," Elaine said.

"Does a non-paying customer count?" Pete needled.

"Hey, now, you could hurt an expert taste-tester's feelings."

"Not a chance," Pete said. He wanted to add that he didn't know she had feelings that could be hurt but thought better of the urge.

"If that horseshoe is supposed to bring good luck, I could use one." Kali said.

"I'll see what I can do."

With Claudia's response, Kali displayed a wide grin. Was he witnessing Kali, the spider, drawing in Claudia, the fly? But for what purpose?

"I can see you are going to make a good addition on Main Street," Kali said, and broke off another bagel piece. "Say, Elaine, why not cut these into bite sizes and let me pass them out with your grand opening flyers? Claudia, you can join me if you have time."

"Good idea," Claudia said. "I'll be free to help after I sort books."

"I can go 'til eleven or so," Kali said. "I've got a business lunch at 11:30, and that two o'clock meeting with you, Pete, at the Hamilton place."

"What's the Hamilton place?" Claudia asked.

"A rundown house Pete is crazy enough to want. It's across the park behind your shop."

"Really?" She looked at Pete who had been on the periphery of the conversation. "I've always thought fixing up an old house would be fun." Claudia said.

Kali shook her head. "Fun? It's more like hard work. Me, I'm for new and ready-to-move-into."

The conversation pinged around Pete. Was he invisible?

"I have to go to The Top of the Harbor apartments to fix a leaky faucet," he said. "I can deliver samples and flyers there, if you'd like."

"Absolutely." Elaine began cutting the bagels into bite sizes. "I hope The Top of the Harbor folks will be some of my best customers." To Claudia and Kali, she said, "You two go ahead, I can sort the books later."

Claudia retrieved a handful of napkins from the storage shelf and handed some to Pete. "Could you stop by my shop and advise me on shelving before your two o'clock meeting?"

Pete opened his mouth to speak, but Kali interjected, "I'll meet you at Claudia's, and we'll walk to the Hamilton house."

Kali made the decision in typical take-over mode. She'd honed the technique to near perfection since high school, and Pete had no desire to argue.

Chapter 4

"O'Flannery," Claudia said, entering her shop, "my luck is changing. I've had a perfect morning with my new friend, Kali."

She patted the little green leprechaun's hat. "No mishaps."

The little statue maintained his perpetual wink. She sighed. "Okay, that is if you don't count knocking over the paint at the bistro."

Claudia selected a doggie print apron with summer flowers and started gathering supplies for her grooming appointment.

Behind her, the shop front door opened, activating a musical recording of "How Much is that Doggie in the Window."

"You don't have a doggie in the window." Pete's face wore his no-nonsense expression. Did a smile ever invade those tough features?

"I plan to have a doggie in the window soon. Thanks for coming by on short notice. This is turning into a great day. The bistro promotion worked out with Kali. Sales is her strong suit. And now you're here."

"Umm ... Kali's a promoter, all right. It's a phenomenon I've witnessed since first grade."

"You've known her that long?"

Pete nodded. "I've seen her charm the principal, the teachers, the janitor ... and everyone else in between. She gets what she wants."

"Elaine couldn't have hired a better promoter. She got commitments to attend the grand opening from merchants and customers on both sides of the street."

"I hope Elaine has a good turnout."

"Kali even offered a free bagel and coffee to a reporter friend, and he agreed to cover the opening. A good idea, don't you think?"

Pete raised a brow. "I think she's mighty quick to offer what's not hers, but ...," he shrugged, "that's Kali." He scrutinized the room. "You wanted shelves?"

So much for friendly conversation. "Yes. Right. I envisioned cubicles like those in the woodworking magazine." Claudia pointed to the wall, left of the front door, "It seems uninteresting to have these wire kennels lined up against the wall. Wouldn't the space look better with colorful small, medium, and large cubes for the cages?" Claudia signed large squares with her hands.

Pete studied the kennels and slowly nodded once, then twice. He took a small notepad from his shirt pocket and unclipped the measuring tape from his belt. He measured the kennels in silence, made some notations, then knelt and measured the length of the wall.

Claudia scooted to hold the end of the tape against the wall for Pete to make his measurement. She withheld chitchat and appraised his rugged good looks. He had interesting line indentions on his cheeks, and his eyes were the color of deep blue water. He stood. His trim waist and broad shoulders didn't go unnoticed either. Then she realized he was trying to retract the tape her knee held down. She pushed up from the floor, and with a loud *ziiip* the tape retracted, caught her foot, and shot the measurer into an open kennel like a hockey puck ringing a noisy score.

"Oh my, did I mess up your tape measure?"

"No problem." Pete retrieved his tape measure, as if it were a perfectly normal place to be, and clipped it on his belt.

Claudia worked to regain her composure, but Pete, unruffled, went straight into his presentation.

"I could build separate cubes of varying sizes. Large cubes would remain on the floor. Above the large cubes, I can mount a shelf to hold smaller cubes for small dogs. Some cubes could be used for merchandise or display items if you like. You could arrange and rearrange them as needed and even paint them a variety of colors."

"Versatile cubes in different colors. As a matter of fact, Izzie Ketterling, who works at The Flower Cottage, suggested brightening the room with something like hot pink and green. Maybe yellow."

Pete gave an affirmative nod. "I think those colors would work."

"Good. But of course, we need to talk price."

"Decide on the number and size of the cubicles, and I'll make a material list and check prices, then give you a proposal. You could always start with enough cubicles for the kennels and make additions as needed."

"Good idea. Give me a start-up price."

The front door opened, tripping the doggie tune again.

"Where's the doggie in the window?" Kali's entry held a presence all its own. She made a neat, professional appearance having added a waist length suit jacket to the trim blue skirt and white blouse she'd worn on their promotion excursion earlier. Pinned to her lapel was a realtor identification tag.

"I guess I need to get a doggie soon," Claudia said. "Pete asked the same thing."

Claudia retrieved a brochure from her appointment table and held it up for Kali and Pete to see. "I'm going to feature animal shelter dogs here. Each dog will hopefully have an increased chance for adoption after they stay in my window a week."

"A worthwhile plan," Pete said. "But I have a feeling you're the type who will want to adopt them all."

"You have me pegged," Claudia said, and returned the brochure to the stack.

"A fine endeavor, but better you than me." Kali scrutinized the puppy pictures on the wall as if examining medical posters in a doctor's office. "How about joining me for dinner at the country club Friday night?" Kali asked Claudia. "I have some people I'd like you to meet who could be a boon to your business."

"Uh ... sure, I'd love to."

"Good." Kali shifted her attention to Pete, who still had his pad and pencil in hand. "Did you get your project here figured out?"

"Good enough."

"Great. Ready to check out your new investment?"

Pete nodded, then closed and tucked the notepad into his shirt pocket.

Kali took the lead and walked toward the back entrance. She parted the romping dog print curtains covering the door glass. "There's Pete's place." She pointed and stepped aside for Claudia to see.

Claudia peered at the old home surrounded by overgrown hedges directly across the park from her shop.

"Hey, that's a good name for the house—Pete's place," Kali said turning to smile at Pete.

"No. The house will keep the Hamilton name," Pete said.

"I guess the original name is best from a historical standpoint." Kali let the curtains fall back in place and snapped her fingers as if just remembering something. "I found out the Downtown Reconstruction Board has plans to renovate Feldman Park and they might add a running trail."

"Wonderful," Claudia said. "My doggie clients love the park, and I love to run."

"More power to you," Kali said. "Running is torture to me. Pete, you still run?"

"I put in five miles every morning."

"Really? We'll both have a handy place to run," Claudia said.

Pete gave a chatter-free nod.

"More important, park improvement will increase property value," Kali said. "Ready to go?"

"I've been ready," Pete said, arms crossed in front of him.

"Okay, I get the hint," Kali said. "I'll talk to you later about what to wear Friday."

Pete opened the door as Kali waved a good-bye and exited. Pete followed. An ever so slight hint of a smile did grace those hard features but not enough to count.

Claudia parted the curtains and watched the two as they made their way past Emme Davenport's renovated Flower Cottage and crossed the park. Though in need of maintenance, the grounds of Feldman Park surrounded by five homes in need of restoration held more than magnificent oak trees but future promise.

Kali gestured with her hands. Pete strode with hands in his pockets. The two were a contrast in personalities. One open, the other reserved. And with the invitation to the country club, Kali could be her ticket to fitting into this community.

Shade from the sprawling oaks broke up a bit of the prickly July heat as Pete and Kali walked across Feldman Park. Pete was bothered by Kali asking Claudia to go to the country club. Why, he wasn't sure. What difference did an invite from Kali to Claudia make? Restoring the Hamilton house should be his only concern.

"What style are these houses?" Kali asked as they made their way across the park. "They look like a conglomeration."

Her question entered his area of expertise. He'd spent many enjoyable hours researching the history and architecture of the homes surrounding Feldman Park. He nodded toward the florist shop on the left corner of the square. "The Flower Cottage is a Craftsman, as is the house next to it. The old Feldman house and its twin across from the florist shop, both are Victorians. The Gardner place is a modified Victorian, and the Hamilton house is a classic American Farmhouse."

"Farmhouse? In the city?"

"In the early 1900s, homes with high ceilings and wrap porches were typical in this part of Florida—a classic style for the farm or in the city."

"Classic run down, if you ask me."

They arrived at the two-and-a-half-story Hamilton house, the dormer windows reflecting the sunlight. Pete's heart lightened, and he rubbed his hands together. The house stood ready to be restored.

"Those front steps don't look very sturdy."

"One of the first items I'll take care of."

"I have to tell you, I wouldn't want to tackle the repairs this place needs, but I know you've got the wherewithal to make the house into a showplace again. We're a little early. Let's go around back."

The roots of a giant oak, draped in moss, lifted the concrete path. "Even walking on this sidewalk is challenging."

"I'll break out the old concrete and construct a new pathway."

Kali raised a brow. "You do concrete work too?" No need to respond. Kali continued her assessment. "There's a one-car garage, with an upstairs you might make into an apartment. And if you trim these shrubs," Kali said pointing to the unruly hedges in the backyard, "you should be able to see the bay." She seemed to be searching for some marketable features.

Pete nodded. "There's a good view of the Harbor Bayou from the second floor."

Kali peered through the massive untended shrubs. "Check this out. There's a little playhouse back here. You'll have the big house to raise a family, and a playhouse for kids. What say you?"

Kali was the last person he'd ever share his personal life with. Pete parted the bushes and looked at the miniature house, which was fashioned as a replica of the big house, right down to the sagging front porch. When new, the little house must have been a favorite place for children. Why have such a big house when all he needed was his one-bedroom apartment? He didn't have an answer.

"Maybe for somebody, but not for me." Pete let the bushes spring closed.

"Why not?"

"My goal is to restore the house."

"Uh huh." She gave him the answer of a skeptic. "If you have this big house restoration to deal with, why take on an extra project with Claudia?"

"I can handle a side job to help Claudia while I restore the Hamilton place."

"And it's just going to be you rambling around in a big old American Farmhouse?"

Pete hesitated, took a deep breath, and said, "Yep."

Kali pulled out a stick lodged in the thick hedges. "I hope to have a family one day, but first I want to try my hand in a big real estate firm. Birmingham has a booming housing market." She tossed the stick to the other side of the yard, trading one messy spot for another.

"You have Birmingham prospects?"

"Not really. Well, sort of ..."

Pete knew Kali. If she wanted something, she'd go after it and use whatever means—or people—necessary.

She flicked at a leaf clinging to her blouse, brushed her hands, and turned back toward the big house. "What I can say with certainty is you have the skills to fix this heap, whatever your whacky reasons. You've made the property arrangement much easier for me. At least I don't have to struggle to put a good face on the deal." Kali looked at her watch. "The Hamilton sisters should be here shortly. We might as well go in."

They made their way to the front of the house and carefully negotiated the rickety steps to the front porch. Kali used the antique key Marigold Hamilton had sent to her to open the front door. It creaked open at her touch.

"Spooky. Sure you don't want to back out?"

"No." Pete cut his eyes toward Kali, who moved aside to let him enter first. "How about you?"

"I'd hire Ghostbusters."

Pete shook his head. "And you call yourself a realtor?" Pete stepped into the entry, which extended into a long dark hallway flanked by stairs to the right, with Kali close on his heels. Maybe she really was scared. The interior held the musty odor of locked up yesterdays. He opened the door on the left to let in some daylight.

"I can't help it, Pete. Old places like this give me the creeps. Maybe I watch too many late-night movies."

Interesting. Kali had a vulnerable spot. "Settle down. Don't you see the charm and potential?"

"I see dust and shadows hiding who knows what."

"I'm anxious to hear what the Hamilton sisters remember about the original house before modifications were made for rental units."

Pete pulled folded papers from his front pocket and opened them for Kali to see. "I made photocopies of some old pictures that I found at the library showing the interior of this house." He pointed to the walled off sections beside the front entry. "It looks like these walls need to come out."

Kali examined the photocopies. "Wow," she said and made a 360-degree inspection. "This area would have been huge, almost the feel of today's great room."

"The entry hall once opened into a parlor on the right. To the left was a study with oversized carved wood pocket doors, partially exposed in this picture. When the doors to these rooms were open, the appearance would have looked like a great room."

"Much of the old *charm*—your word, not mine—has definitely been buried."

Pete stepped into the vacant apartment to the right. Kali stuck close. Their footsteps echoed. Kali ran her finger over the fireplace mantel and wrinkled her nose at the puff of dislodged dust. "So, at some point you'll restore these rooms to their former magnificence, but I still can't see going to all the work for just one person to live here."

At the thud of car doors closing, Pete moved to the front window and saw two women beginning to navigate the sidewalk covered with grass and weeds. One of the sisters, round and plump, waddled duck-like with abbreviated steps on short, stumpy legs. The other woman, in contrast, was taller—maybe five-and-a-half-feet tall and slender. Posture erect, she walked with a slight limp, used a cane, and carried a tube container in her free hand.

Kali joined Pete at the window.

"We better help them up the steps," Pete said.

43

Kali agreed and followed.

"Good day, ladies." Kali gave them a cheerful greeting.

"Let me give you a hand," Pete said.

"Certainly not," the tall one replied and tipped her nose a couple of degrees. "Hurry up Petunia," she said, giving her sister a nudge.

"Speak for yourself, Marigold." She lifted her lavender-tinted eyes and tossed her mop of blue-tinted curls. "I could use some help."

Pete offered his arm to Petunia while Marigold used her cane with precision to negotiate the steps. Neither Kali nor Pete dared offering her more assistance.

"You must be the realtor," Marigold said, reaching the top of the steps.

"Yes, ma'am. I'm Kali Reppen, with Southern Realty. We've talked on the phone." She motioned toward Pete. "This is Pete Cullen."

Pete stepped forward and stretched out his hand to Marigold. She gave his hand a brisk, firm shake. "Marigold Hamilton, and this is my sister, Petunia."

Petunia reached out both plump hands, encircled Pete's, and shook them vigorously. "Nice to meet you, and we're delighted you want to restore Granddaddy's house."

"Well, let's get on with the legalities." Marigold pointed to the front door with her cane like a military commander issuing orders.

When they stepped inside the house, Petunia let out a great sigh. "Oh sister, everything looks so … so …"

"Like a dump." Marigold finished whatever her sister was trying to express.

"The rundown appearance will all change. And you'll have the best working for you when you sign on with Pete," Kali said. "Shall we go to the kitchen where we can spread out the paperwork?"

The kitchen, with its ten-foot ceiling, had large windows above the cabinets that allowed the sun to light the room. Pete dusted off an old porcelain-topped worktable with his handkerchief, and Kali spread out legal papers. The group discussed the specific terms of the contract. If Pete satisfactorily restored the home and grounds to the original design and met a specific contingency to be announced, he could purchase the home at 15% below market value.

With the paperwork approved, Marigold opened one end of the tube she carried and pulled out some yellowed papers. "I thought you might be interested in the original house plans."

If she had dumped a roll of gold coins onto the table, Pete couldn't have been more ecstatic.

"You bet."

Pete examined the drawings, and Marigold pointed out where walls and bathrooms had been added to make five rental units. "Two downstairs and three upstairs. The renters shared access to the hallways and kitchen. These plans show the original library and parlor on the first floor. There was a master bedroom and bath and two smaller bedrooms, with a connecting bath, on the second floor. The third level was used as a children's play area and doubled as a guest bedroom."

"Daddy used to have his model train railroad on the third floor." Petunia pulled several old photos from her purse and spread them on the table. She pointed to two little girls seated on a porch swing. "Marigold and me on the front porch," she said. "But our favorite spot was here." She presented a picture of the two girls standing arm-in-arm in front of the playhouse outside. "The playhouse will be part of the restoration." Pete could see Marigold wasn't always the one in charge.

Kali caught Pete's eye and winked. "The playhouse is part of the grounds."

Pete tried to ignore her now-you've-got-to-fix-the-playhouse look and said, "I'll see the playhouse is restored just like the photo."

"Renting the houses on Feldman Square worked quite nicely for a few years until the upkeep became more than the rent," Marigold said. "When we took jobs out of state, closing the houses became the easiest thing to do."

"But we don't want this or any of the houses to be an eye-sore—or worse—torn down," Petunia said, pushing her lips into a pout.

"Restoration seems the answer. We want to start with this house, and make it look like the original. Understood?" Marigold spoke with a boldness and clarity Pete appreciated.

"Understood."

"The Flower Cottage on the corner has been renovated, but yellow and green aren't the original colors," Marigold said with a sniff.

"The florist shop was built for Daddy's sister, you know." Petunia moved to the edge of her chair, close to the blueprints. "And there's something you must see that is interesting about all the houses Granddaddy built on the square."

"That will wait, sister." The sharpness of Marigold's retort could have snipped a tough flower stem. Petunia wilted.

"There's a specific contingency we'll discuss with you, Mr. Cullen. No need to waste Miss Reppen's time." Marigold said.

Kali stood and looked at her watch. "I have another appointment. I'll get the contract copied and mailed as agreed. The contingency can be added as an amendment later, if you like." She gathered the signed papers. "Ladies, if you'll excuse me? Pete, I'll see you later."

"Thanks for your help."

The sound of Kali's heels echoed down the long hallway. The front door rattled closed, and Petunia edged back up to the table.

With violet-colored eyes suddenly quite vivid, she focused on Pete and said, "There's a secret room you have to find."

Chapter 5

The morning sun brightened the rear section of the grooming shop. The time was 7:50, and all was quiet at The Pampered Pooch, except for a chortling bird concert coming from Feldman Park. The happy sounds sweetening Claudia's new residence contrasted with the honking car horns and wailing sirens that introduced the beginning of day in Atlanta. She breathed in, let the tranquility flood her soul, prayed for a successful opening day for Elaine, and thanked God for the two frisky clients expected shortly.

A series of raps rattled the glass on the shop's front door and interrupted her gathering of grooming supplies. Was Ms. Appleberry early?

Hurrying to the front, Claudia recognized Kali peering through the door glass, holding up two bistro logo cups, her blonde hair the picture of perfection. Claudia adjusted the headband on her own disorderly curls and unlocked the deadbolt. "Good morning. What brings you my way?"

"I missed seeing you at Elaine's, so I brought a latte Elaine said is your favorite."

"How sweet. Come in." Claudia accepted the coffee, flipped on the "Doggie in the Window" recording, and motioned Kali to take a seat on the sofa by the front door. Above the small couch, Claudia had hung some alluring puppy posters to break up the long expanse of wall.

"I figured you'd be helping Elaine with her grand opening, but she seems to have things under control."

"I offered, but she assured me she'd be fine with her college student helper. I finished shelving books for the lending library last night."

Claudia tried a sip of coffee. Too hot. "As it turns out, I have clients coming this morning, and my aunt from Tallahassee is stopping by. She knows Elaine from our college days and wants to be here for the bistro's grand opening."

"Good. Elaine's restaurant is going to be a boon for all of the businesses downtown."

"I guess we will all benefit." Claudia took the lid off, blew on her coffee, and tried another sip.

"When do you expect your customer?" Kali asked.

"The appointment is for eight." Claudia glanced at her watch, 8:10. "Mrs. Appleberry should be here already."

Kali wrinkled her brow and slid forward to the edge of the seat, cupping her coffee in both hands. "About tomorrow …"

She seemed uneasy. Had she been too hasty to invite her to the country club? "Was there something you needed to tell me?"

"Well … tomorrow night at the country club, do you mind if I introduce you as a dog trainer?"

"Dog trainer?" Claudia flinched, sloshing coffee on her hand and the floor.

Kali grabbed some paper towels from the grooming supplies and wiped at the spill on the table and floor while Claudia ran cool water on her hand at the sink.

"Why would you want to introduce me as a dog trainer?" Claudia toweled her hand dry.

Kali's confidence visibly waned. She crumpled and tossed the wad of coffee-soaked paper into the trashcan. Was she searching for the right words? "It's just … dog trainer has a nice ring. Elaine said you used to train dogs?"

"I did, but—"

The corners of Kali's mouth upturned. "Perfect."

Claudia's heart pounded in her chest. Flashing visions of cold, hard handcuffs thrust on her wrists and posing for front and side view pictures dogged her. "Kali, 'used to' are the operative words. I—"

"How Much is that Doggie in the Window" interrupted their conversation. Two white bichons burst into the shop with a disheveled Olivia Appleberry, double leash in hand. All three panted.

"Sorry I'm late." With her blouse sagged off one shoulder, Olivia's hair was askew, and her cheeks were flushed a bright pink.

Kali closed the door.

Claudia knelt to pet the hyper dogs. "Did they give you a rough time this morning?"

"Just a minute," Olivia said. She handed the leash to Claudia and plunked her plump figure on the couch. "Let me catch my breath." She pulled a paper from her purse, fanned herself, and pushed her short, brown curls from her damp face.

Claudia unhooked one of the fluffy, overfed dogs, and handed the leash holding the other dog to Kali.

"This is Fritz, right?" Claudia asked.

"The one and only." Olivia increased her fanning speed.

Claudia scratched the dog behind the ears and took him to one of the kennels.

"Olivia, you know Kali Reppen from Southern Realty?"

"We've never been formally introduced, but I've seen you around."

"Hi," Kali extended her hand. "You and your husband run the furniture store up the street?"

"Sure do. And we have a sale going on this week." She offered the hand not fanning her face. "Pleased to meet you, and thanks for holding onto Corky."

Kali held the leash but kept her distance from the dog.

"Hi there, Corky," Kali said. Corky let out a low grumble. Kali took a half-step backward. "Don't worry boy, I'm not messing with you."

"Corky, behave. Best put Corky in the kennel with Fritz," Olivia said. She tugged at her shirt to straighten it on her shoulders. "If you don't, they'll both yelp and drive you batty."

Claudia complied.

With the dogs kenneled, Kali returned to her normal self. "Ladies, I have to get to the office. Nice meeting you, Olivia." She made her exit. Corky and Fritz yapped after her.

"The boys were bad this morning," Olivia said, wiping her forehead with the back of her hand. "I got Fritz in the car, then Corky ran to the neighbor's yard. When I got him back, Fritz had escaped."

Claudia laughed and observed the dogs' benign expressions peeking through the kennel bars. "Maybe they'll rest and enjoy their spa treatment and give you a break."

"I hope so. My husband brought this flyer home." She unfolded the paper-turned-fan, and Claudia recognized the flyer from the bistro. "After I run errands, I'm meeting him for lunch at the grand opening and ordering the tallest, coldest Frappuccino they serve."

"One of my best friends from college owns the bistro. I plan to have your boys bathed and groomed before lunch so I can attend the grand opening too. You want to keep them kenneled until later this afternoon?"

"Works for me."

Claudia sprayed a little citrus grooming scent on her arm for Olivia to sniff. "New after-bath doggie spritz. What do you think?"

Olivia sniffed and rolled her eyes as if the spray was a designer fragrance. "I love the personal attention you've given the brothers since taking over this grooming shop." She dabbed at the last of the perspiration on her forehead.

"I aim to please. Taking on The Pampered Pooch has been exciting but a little scary. With franchise pet stores opening north of town, I had to take the risk that people would still be willing to bring their pets downtown."

"Don't you worry. I'll help get word out."

"Thank you." According to Elaine, Olivia's ability to spread news could challenge a billboard. Claudia walked Olivia to the door. "Listen. Dogs are welcome on the outside patio at the bistro. I can bring them to you, if you like."

"Oh, would you? Delivering Fritz and Corky is a personal service I can't turn down. I'll see you there."

Olivia opened the door, setting off the doggie tune, and collided with Claudia's short, wiry Aunt Lucy.

"Oh my, I'm so sorry I didn't see you there." Olivia said.

"It's okay," Aunt Lucy chuckled. "I'm still in one piece." She gripped a cluster of white flowers in one hand and straightened her T-shirt adorned with a picture of hiking boots with her other hand. "Dumplin,' you always loved my gardenias," she held up the bouquet, "I picked these for you."

"Thank you." Claudia gave her aunt a hug. "Aunt Lucy, meet Mrs. Appleberry. I'm grooming her bichons."

"Good to meet you." Aunt Lucy pumped Olivia's hand.

"Same here." Olivia rubbed her wrist after the handshaking. "Hope the boys are good for you," she called over her shoulder and hurried to her car.

Claudia ushered Aunt Lucy into her shop. "Love your T-shirt. Where's your volksmarching group walking next?" Aunt Lucy might be sixty-five, but she could outwalk most fifty-year-olds.

"Pensacola. I'll head over there after Elaine's grand opening. How is she doing?"

"I've yet to taste a bad bagel sample. You're going to love her new place. Her mocha coffee with sweet cream is to die for."

Aunt Lucy shook her head and laughed. "That sounds seriously good. I'm happy for her. What about you?" Her eyes settled on Corky and Fritz. "You have two well-behaved customers."

"They're mischievous at times."

Corky and Fritz perked up their ears.

"Aren't we all?" Aunt Lucy gave Claudia a spirited wink.

"I have something to show you." Claudia opened the magazine on her appointment table and flipped to the bookmarked page with the shelving. "The guy remodeling Elaine's bistro is giving me a price to build shelving similar to this."

Arm outstretched, Aunt Lucy took the magazine. She rotated in a semicircle as she looked at the bare walls and studied the picture. "Splendid idea."

Confidence rose in Claudia. Aunt Lucy had an eye for decorating. If she liked something, she told you. The same was true if she didn't.

"Where are my manners? You must be tired after your drive. Don't you want to rest for a while before we go to the opening?"

"No thanks, dear. The drive wasn't bad, but I could use your ladies' room."

"Upstairs and to the right."

Aunt Lucy took to the stairs with a bounce in her step. Thankfully, tripping on Claudia's shoes and breaking her hip during Claudia's middle-school years didn't leave permanent damage.

Claudia found an empty vase for the gardenias. She placed them on her appointment table. Closing her eyes, she drew in a deep breath, and the sweet smell took her back to the porch at Gramma's house.

"Marlene, I can't keep up. Is this anniversary number fourteen or fifteen?" Aunt Lucy, her dad's aunt and her grandmother's younger sister, asked as she settled into a rocker with her knitting.

"Fifteen," Mom answered.

Gramma sat in her usual spot on the porch swing. "Marlene, Claudia sure is accident-prone."

"Why do you say that?" The chains holding the porch swing screeched as Gramma leaned forward. "The girl knocks stuff over, throws up on trips, fell off the fishing boat ..."

Claudia stared at the sticky hummingbird food drying on the porch step. What Gramma said was true. She did bump into things. At least the feeder was plastic. She managed to get out of the car before she threw up this time. And she was just trying to hold the net for her Dad's fish when she fell off the boat. It wasn't like she wanted to be sick or clumsy. What could she do?

"She's just hit a growth spurt, and lots of kids get car sick. She'll outgrow it," her mother said.

"My Italian grandmother would hang a bulb of garlic around her neck." Gramma said. "She might not live long enough to outgrow her hard luck."

"Why on earth? Garlic around the neck?" Claudia's mother asked.

Gramma pushed back in the swing then stopped its movement. "Garlic is supposed to ward off misfortune and evil."

"Poppycock." Aunt Lucy said. "All garlic would do is make it hard for Claudia to make friends."

Claudia stared at her grandmother. Didn't she know she was sitting there? Gramma's foreboding upset her stomach again.

"Maybe ballet lessons, or etiquette classes." Gramma suggested.

"Hush that kind of talk," Aunt Lucy yanked at her yarn and picked up her knitting speed. The needles clicked in rapid fire. "You're the one who needs etiquette classes."

"Just trying to offer some helpful ideas." [End letter/Scripture indent]

Corky yipped, or was it Fritz? Claudia opened her eyes. Gramma got her chance at a makeover for Claudia with ballet and etiquette classes. But after Claudia knocked over the background scenery during a dance recital, even Gramma gave up.

Aunt Lucy returned, "You seem deep in thought."

"I guess I was. The gardenias brought back memories of Gramma's house."

"Ah. Yes. She had beautiful gardenia bushes around her porch."

"Remember when Gramma talked about the garlic necklace?"

"I do."

"I wanted to have a fresh start here, but my black cloud still hovers."

Aunt Lucy patted her hand. "Honey, just be willing to look for the silver lining."

"Oh. I'm more than willing."

"Good. Now, put me to work."

The bichon boys stood and wagged. Corky put a paw on his brother's neck. Fritz nipped at Corky's ear, starting a playful tussle.

Something told Claudia she needed to accept Aunt Lucy's offer of help.

"Pete Cullen. You made this for me?"

Dressed in khaki slacks and a bistro T-shirt, Elaine stretched on tiptoe, pulled Pete down to her level, and gave him a hug. She clasped her hands together and inspected the A-frame sign on wheels that Pete had positioned in front of the restaurant.

"I thought a sign for the sidewalk would be a good way to advertise your daily specials."

"A portable sign. It's absolutely perfect."

Harbor Town Bagel Bistro was stenciled on the top in eye-catching gold-on-green acrylic lettering. "I printed 'Grand Opening' on the whiteboard." Pete handed her a package of different colored dry erase markers. "You can add what you like."

"I know just what to write." Elaine pulled out a green pen and wrote, "National Hot Dog Month, Try our Bagel Dog Special." As she moved to write on the other side, Pete saw Elaine's husband and daughters approaching.

Jeff put a finger to his lips. Pete kept silent. When Jeff got right behind Elaine, he said, "You know a decent place to get a cup of coffee around here?"

Elaine jerked, sending a green streak across the whiteboard. Her startled expression melted into a loving grin. "Jeff, I thought you had to work, and your mom was keeping the girls."

"Nope," Jeff said. "Mom will be here later."

"We con … What was it we did?" Cindy asked.

"Conspired," Jeff said.

Cindy raised expressive hands. "We conspired."

"That means our surprise was a secret," Mara said.

"And you kept your secret well." Elaine knelt and wrapped her arms around her girls.

"I took the day off. Since we agreed this is a team effort, the girls and I wanted to be here. Right, girls?"

"Yes," both girls chimed in and huddled close to their mom.

Pete's heart clouded with longing. What would it be like to be a part of a close-knit family and have daughters to share secrets with?

"Look at what Pete made for me. Isn't the sign terrific?"

Pete grimaced with the spotlight on him. "I just put some old scraps of wood together."

"You know how to handle scraps pretty well." Jeff shook Pete's hand.

Mara pulled a pink marker from the package. "Oh boy. Mommy, can we draw?"

"Maybe later." Elaine erased her stray mark and finished writing the day's special. "Emme and Izzie dropped by earlier with flowers and balloons. They had a job conflict and couldn't stay. I was disappointed, but I'm so glad you're here. Girls," she led them to a table beside the bistro entry, "I copied the flyers you made and put coupons on the bottom." Elaine gave each girl a small stack of flyers. "Your job today, ladies, is to give every customer a flyer and ask them to come back."

Fwap!

Elaine grabbed the loose end of the "Opening Soon" banner and rolled her eyes. "I'd hoped this sign would hang on for the day."

"Never fear, your fix-it men are here," Jeff said in a valiant tone.

"My poetic hero," Elaine stroked Jeff's cheek in exaggerated appreciation. "I'll get the duct tape."

Pete took in the sweet scene, and it pricked a tender spot in his heart. He retrieved and positioned the ladder under the drooping banner.

"I appreciate all your help, Pete." Jeff pulled off strips of tape and handed them to Pete as needed. "Opening her own place has been a dream of Elaine's for a long time. I hope this celebration goes well."

"She's fortunate to have your support." Loving encouragement, once his dream, he'd accepted as unrealistic for him.

The WHIZ radio van wheeled into a reserved space in front of the bistro.

"Elaine's radio promo has arrived." Jeff beamed like a proud parent. "Another step closer to being officially open."

"Hopefully, the banner will stay fastened during the ceremony. I'll put this ladder away."

When Pete returned, a reporter from the *Hamilton Harbor Daily News* was interviewing Elaine, a local television newscaster was setting up video equipment, and Mayor Brimstead had arrived with his ribbon and supersized scissors.

"Pete," a voice hailed. Pete knew the voice from his work with the Helping Hands Ministry at the church. Dave Burbank approached with Francine Waterman and two others.

"You got connections for a front row seat at this shindig?" His voice boomed from his craggy face lined by long days of work in the hot sun as a Florida Marine Patrol officer.

"Would you stop?" Francine said in good-humored annoyance. "You make Pete out to be some sort of maître d'. Pete, I want you to meet my friends, Lake and Mallory Spencer." She lowered her voice to a whisper. "They're private investigators."

Pete exchanged handshakes. The couple in their 60s had brown hair, easy smiles, and could blend in most anywhere, which probably worked to their advantage.

"Pete is our Mr. Fix-it." Francine added.

"Good man to know," Mallory said.

"I do what I can, and I'll be glad to play maître d' for you three." Pete cut his eyes toward Dave. "Dave, here, is a different story."

Dave raised caterpillar look-alike brows over twinkling eyes. If Pete didn't needle Dave about his teasing ways, he'd be disappointed.

"Folks are arriving. Let's see what's available." Pete led them to the outdoor seating. Several of the wrought iron tables were already claimed. They took a table for six near the sound system and mayor.

"Elaine plans to serve free bagel samples after the ribbon-cutting," Pete said.

Dave winked. "Free eats are why we're here."

"And, of course, to support Elaine," Francine said, and thanked Pete for pulling out her chair.

"Oh, yeah, and to support Elaine too." Dave shot a smug look at Pete.

"We need to support anyone who takes time and effort to help rebuild downtown," Francine said.

"She'll appreciate you being here," Pete adjusted the large canvas umbrella to give them more shade.

Red curly hair, made brilliant in the noonday sun, caught Pete's eye. Claudia approached with what appeared to be two giant fluffed-out Swiffer dusters on a double leash. An older lady, with short, salt-and-pepper gray hair, kept pace with the trio, arms swinging with each stride.

Dave leaned toward Francine and her friends and lowered his voice. "Speaking of building downtown, there's the girl that bought the dog grooming shop. She was at church Wednesday night."

"I saw her there. Seems to be a nice young lady," Francine said and eyed Pete. Her look came across as one that included a rose-covered cottage, white picket fence, and clanging wedding bells.

"Yes, she does." Dave said in a conspiratorial tone, bushy brows pushed together.

"You two can stop with your not-so-subtle hints." Some men apparently carried the matchmaking gene too.

Pete stole a look in Claudia's direction as she handed the dogs over to a couple seated at a table.

Her eyes met Pete's. She flashed him a grin and walked toward him with her companion. "Well, here is someone I know," Claudia said. She introduced her Aunt Lucy. "Pete is the one helping me with the shelving project in my shop."

Aunt Lucy scrutinized Pete with her near-black eyes and gave him a solid handshake. After introductions were made, Pete asked, "Who are your furry friends?"

"Two freshly groomed bichons that belong to Olivia Appleberry. She and her husband run the furniture store up the street. Corky is the large one. Fritz the smaller. Both are a handful."

"We are so glad to have you as a neighbor," Dave said. "Please, sit with us."

Claudia and Aunt Lucy took the remaining seats.

"Dave and I have apartments in The Top of the Harbor high rise on the marina at the end of Main Street," Francine said. "Anybody who opens a business downtown, we claim as neighbors."

"I'm privileged to be considered your neighbor."

"We apartment dwellers just call our building The Top." Dave dragged a chair from another table next to Claudia. "Pete, you sit here."

"Did I hear somebody mention The Top?" Kali walked up and inserted herself into the conversation.

The radio announcer's voice, signaling the beginning of the ceremony, rose above the noise of fifty or so people.

"Okay if I sit with you?" Kali took the empty chair beside Claudia before anyone responded.

Pete slipped his hands into his pockets. Odd man out.

"Pete, pull up a chair on the other side of Claudia," Dave said.

Casting Dave his "don't-press" look, Pete pulled up a chair across from Claudia.

The television cameraman started filming and the WHIZ radio announcer spoke. "Welcome to folks here, and to our radio listeners. We are live on location at the grand opening of the new Harbor Town Bagel Bistro."

The ribbon the mayor brought had been stretched from one side of the wrought iron fence to the bistro's entry door.

"To help kick things off, we have Mayor Brimstead."

Enthusiastic applause honored the well-loved mayor. Badly burned and disfigured in Vietnam, the heavy-set mayor needed a cane to walk. Leaning on his cane with one hand, he accepted the microphone with the other.

"It is indeed a pleasure to stand here and witness the opening of another new business in downtown Hamilton Harbor. Our town, established in 1912, is getting its second wind, thanks to entrepreneurs like Elaine Robinson and her bagel bistro. She tells me this is National Hot Dog month, and today the bistro is the place to celebrate. Ms. Robinson is offering free bagel-dog samples."

A bark punctuated the word "samples."

"Well, looky here." Mayor Brimstead said, "How fitting. Two real dogs have joined us."

Corky's attention appeared to be somewhere behind the mayor. He let out a high-pitched yip and tugged at the leash, jerking the chair a good six inches. Fritz sprung to his feet. He produced a series of staccato barks that rivaled a jackhammer and lunged.

The dual leash snapped loose.

Olivia grabbed, but came up with nothing but air.

Pete pointed at a sleek black flash of fur.

Claudia jumped up. "It's that cat again."

The radio announcer grabbed the microphone and started a running narration. "Live from the downtown bistro, the chase is on. Two dogs against one cat. Turn on the music, it looks like a revival of the "Bristol Stomp" from the 60s with spectators trying to trap the leashes of the runaway dogs. They're headed for the stretched-out ribbon. Oh no! Mayor Brimstead! Your cane—"

The microphone recorded a loud clank followed by a static squeal that had onlookers clamping their hands over their ears. The mayor, who landed in a chair, was laughing so hard the paramedics might have had to be called. The news reporter was on his knees reaching for the screeching microphone.

The cat scampered behind Pete's sign. Corky darted to the left, Fritz to the right, and the cat shot straight up like a cannon ball.

In one jump, the cat leaped over the bistro's wrought iron fencing, sank her claws into the grand opening banner and swung out over the crowd. With the leash, the ribbon, and the portable sign holding them back, Corky and Fritz struggled to follow. The air filled with spirited yelps and barking.

"You boys get back here right now," Olivia shrieked. Their barking volume increased.

Headed for the corridor, the devilish feline streaked past.

"Corky. Fritz." Claudia's voice, calm yet firm, quieted the dogs. She worked to untangle the web of ribbon and leash wound about the chairs and Pete's sign.

"Let's get the banner off the patrons," Jeff said to Pete.

"Sorry, so sorry. Sorry," Olivia said. Followed by her husband, she made her way to retrieve the dogs.

Claudia rubbed the fur between Corky's eyes and tickled Fritz under his chin. "You fellas finished with all the excitement?"

Jeff straightened table umbrellas. Pete stopped folding the banner. He was mesmerized by Claudia's calming ability, as were other bystanders.

"How did you get them to sit like that?" Olivia asked. "When they get off on one of their tangents, it takes me forever to settle them down."

Claudia shrugged. Olivia and her husband grasped their strong-willed dogs and continued to apologize.

Elaine used a menu to fan the mayor, perspiring in the summer heat. Mayor Brimstead retrieved his cane and pushed himself up from the chair. "Everyone ... please ..."

The crowd settled down and refocused on the mayor. "In recognition of National Hot Dog Month, and with the assistance of some real dogs, I declare this new business in our great city of Hamilton Harbor officially open. Let's all have one of those bagel dogs!"

The crowd cheered, and Corky and Fritz wagged freshly washed and fluffed tails.

"Impressive," Pete said to Claudia.

"Impressive disrupter." Her eyes glistened and chin trembled. "What's with me, dogs, and the bistro?"

"Surely you don't think the dogs' romp is your fault?"

"I brought the dogs here."

"And you masterfully got them calmed down."

"You certainly did," Kali said, hooking her arm with Claudia's. "Come with me. I want you to meet someone."

Kali introduced her to Lyman Beardsley, reporter for the local *Talk of the Town* weekly newspaper. He wore a Panama straw hat with a press card stuck in the hatband. Displaying the press label struck Pete as an effort to legitimize the stories he managed to put a sensational spin on.

While Kali made chummy conversation with Claudia and Lyman, Pete accepted a flyer from Cindy, finished folding the banner, and set it aside.

Maybe he should be relieved to get a reprieve from matchmakers, Francine and Dave, but Pete couldn't help wondering why Kali had taken such an interest in Claudia—a dog groomer. Not that dog grooming was an unworthy profession, but the Kali he knew attached herself to people for personal gain. Kali didn't own a dog.

He picked up the eraser for Elaine's sign that had fallen to the pavement and wished he could use it to rub out his discontent. He didn't want the bubbly redhead to get hurt.

Chapter 6

The phone rang. Claudia froze. The digital clock registered 5:30 a.m. Something must be wrong. She grabbed the phone and checked the caller ID. Elaine.

"What's wrong?"

"We've gone viral!"

"What?"

"Viral—the internet—I just got a call from the national affiliate to our local TV station." Elaine's words ran together.

"Slow down. I didn't get much sleep after yesterday's fiasco."

"Listen to me," Elaine tried to speak slowly. "Because of the fiasco, the bichon brothers have made my bistro famous."

"Famous?"

"You heard me. Somebody posted the video of yesterday's doggie romp on YouTube. The TV network picked up on the story and wants to do a human interest report."

"At this hour?"

"I guess news people work around the clock. We made the front page of the Hamilton Harbor newspaper too."

Claudia wedged the phone between her ear and shoulder, pushed the mop of hair from her eyes, scrambled to her feet and trotted downstairs.

The morning paper lay on the shop floor by the mail drop. She stared at the bold black print on the front page.

Grrrrand Opening Dog-Gone Grrrreat.

The story featured a picture of Elaine and the mayor standing on one side of Pete's sidewalk sign. Corky and Fritz, tongues hanging out and still decorated with a tangle of grand opening ribbon, sat on the other side.

"Would you believe? They want to do a live interview."

"Who does?"

"The local television affiliate. I never could have come up with that kind of advertising. I owe my new found fame to you."

"Are you saying the free-for-all that wrecked your grand opening was a good thing?"

"I was afraid you'd convince yourself that you brought me bad luck yesterday. I had to let you know everything turned out to be a blessing. Got to go. Bagels to bake."

Claudia's bare feet thumped against the hardwood stairs. In her kitchen, she plugged in her coffee pot, prepped the night before, and sat down to read the article.

> Here's a business truly gone to the dogs. The new Harbor Town Bagel Bistro had a unique grand opening. In honor of National Hot Dog Month, the new business featured free bagel dogs. Two real adorable bichons, Corky and Fritz, showed up to help celebrate. They gave a new twist to live advertising gimmicks, and these cute canines showed they could handle the job. All they needed was a little feline incentive.

There were interview remarks from Elaine, who spoke of her love for baking and the hope of being a part of downtown's revival. The mayor said the grand opening was "the dog-gonedist" he'd ever attended. Apologetic for her dogs' behavior, Olivia Appleberry said, "At least they looked good. I just had them groomed at The Pampered Pooch."

Claudia smiled. "Bless Ms. Olivia."

The coffee pot's gurgling stopped. Claudia poured a cup and resettled at the table. She had to admit, the bichon brothers on the front page did look well-groomed. She thought about Aunt Lucy's admonition to look for the positive. The news interest *was* a silver lining for yesterday's black cloud.

After finishing a quick breakfast of toast and soft-boiled egg, Claudia was nearing the three-mile mark on the treadmill when she heard a rap at the shop door. She grabbed a towel and dabbed at the perspiration on her face and arms. It was early for her first grooming appointment.

She bounded downstairs. Pete, looking mighty dashing, was framed in the shop door glass. Behind him, foot and car traffic seemed unusually busy.

"Good morning. You caught me just getting off the treadmill." Claudia draped the towel about her neck. "I'll be glad when the weather cools off a bit, so I can run outside. Did you put in your five miles?"

"I did."

"You'll have to fill me in on good places to run." Claudia paused. A car passed by, then another. "What's with the traffic?"

"The bistro." He spoke as though interest growing overnight was the norm.

Claudia's eyes widened. "You're kidding." She stepped back for him to enter.

"I don't kid. I was just down there. The place is bustling."

"Elaine called and said the local television affiliate called for an interview." Claudia touched her cheeks with both hands. "I was afraid I ruined everything. Is it possible I didn't jinx things after all?"

Pete raised his eyebrows. "You?"

"I'm the one who suggested taking the dogs to the grand opening."

"So?"

"So ... so ... uh ... undesirable things happen when I'm around. You know. I knocked you off your ladder." She lowered her voice and mumbled, "Spilled over the polyurethane finish, didn't lock your toolbox—put you in harm's way." She pointed at Pete's bandaged hand.

His azure eyes settled on her. "I think you're taking credit where none is due."

She could stand to spend some time soaking in the blue of those eyes.

Pete motioned to the folder secured under his arm. "I brought some drawings and cost estimates."

Business. The guy was all business.

"Great. Bring them over here." Claudia tugged Pete's arm. The folder fell to the floor and papers scattered.

"Good grief." Claudia dropped to her knees and helped gather the contents of the folder. "Me and my bad—" She wouldn't say it.

Not commenting on her blunder, Pete reorganized the drawings and spread the papers on the platform.

Claudia relaxed.

"I can build cubicles of varying sizes for your kennels as we discussed. One could frame your humane shelter pet of the week." He showed her a sketch depicting a window display. "You could exchange the small appointment table for a cube table and replace the legs on your sofa with a cube base if you wanted to coordinate more."

Pete surprised her. His speech held an enthusiasm missing when he spoke in general conversation. Even his body language took on a new fervor. "Perhaps patterns could be mixed with solid colors."

"You're a genius. These plans line up with Izzie's ideas. But I need to consider cost before I get too excited."

Pete handed her a proposal sheet. "The price of the different size cubes includes material and labor."

"Your prices seem reasonable. Can you start with the ones you proposed for the window display and the kennel wall?"

"Fine." His no-frills responses reminded her of Aunt Lucy.

"Maybe I can afford to have the others made later. When can you begin?"

"I have some other projects to work around, but I can gather the materials to start on yours today."

"Do you need a deposit?"

"No. Pay me when the project is complete and you're satisfied."

"It's a deal then?" Claudia held out her hand to seal the agreement with a shake. His handshake was solid and firm and sent unexpected warmth all the way up her arm to her cheeks.

Pete parked his truck loaded with materials for Claudia's project near the back entrance of The Pampered Pooch and got out. A mixed canopy of puffy white and solemn gray clouds hung over the Hamilton home across the park. He'd not only achieved his teenage goal to see the inside of the house, but now he might live there.

And yet? And yet what? Why no joy? His quandary was like trying to come up with a word that almost crystallizes, then evaporates before becoming clear.

He rubbed the back of his neck. The questions tumbled about his mind. Was it Claudia's cheery face and flaming hair behind his restless spirit? He needed to shake off his discontent and concentrate on the job at hand.

The smell of new wood from the back of his truck stirred his creative juices and helped the nagging questions to stop.

Pete knocked on the back door. After a moment, Claudia peeked through the curtains, smiled in recognition and opened the door. She was wearing a pink ruffled work apron covered with an assortment of paw prints. The front of the apron was soaking wet. Her hair, piled atop her head, lit up in the sunlight. It reminded him of the blazing orange sunsets over the Gulf of Mexico he had appreciated from the oil drilling platform.

"Hi," she said, a bit out of breath. "You caught me working out again." She motioned to her elevated dog-washing tub that held a forlorn-looking dog. "My workout today is coming from a not-too-happy Afghan hound who hates his bath."

"He looks like he lost his best friend."

Claudia laughed. "You're right. But wait 'til I'm through with him. He'll perk up."

"I've got two hours and the materials to get started."

"You don't waste time. Just come and go as you need." Claudia stepped back for Pete to enter.

"How do you get the hound to stand still for you?"

"I use a neck and belly restraint," she said returning to the bedraggled dog.

"Hey, boy." Pete spoke to the dog as he passed by him. "She assures me you'll feel better soon." The dog, shivering and tail between his legs, stared at him through a veil of wet stringy hair. To Claudia, he said, "I'll take some final measurements, and set up sawhorses out back so I don't make a mess in here."

"Good idea." The green in her eyes sparkled when she spoke—her smile accentuated dimpled indentions on her cheeks and an array of tiny freckles across her nose. She looked fresh in sharp contrast to the wet mop of a dog in front of her.

Pete set to work. Intermittently, his interest strayed to Claudia as she combed, brushed, dried, and trimmed the dog. She had large hands and feet. But the combination seemed just right on her and gave her the ability to produce a perfectly groomed dog.

"You are beautiful, Mister T." She framed the Afghan's face with her hands. "The T stands for terrific, doesn't it, fella?"

The dog waggled and lifted his chest. Claudia had changed him from ragged to regal.

"Cute, isn't he?"

"He looks a lot better dry than wet."

Claudia grinned, led the hound to a large kennel, and rattled the lock into place. When she turned around, she yelped. "You've finished a storage cube for the window already?"

She moved toward the shop window. "Oops." Claudia's apron had snagged on the kennel lock.

"Back up. I'll unhook you."

She did, stepped on Pete's foot, and fell against him. A sweet, citrusy smell pricked his senses.

"I'm so sorry."

He wasn't. "No problem. I wear steel-toe boots." Her hair tickled his chin, making his skin rise in little bumps. He busied himself unhooking the apron.

"Good thing with me around." Her lips pressed into a tight line, she re-tied her apron and then examined his handiwork.

"Amazing." She ran her hand over the wood, as if the simple cubical was expensive cabinetry.

"The cube will look better with acrylic paint. I thought I'd use high-gloss colors for the window displays."

"I trust your judgment." She put an index finger to her mouth. Her eyes glinted as the sun streaked through the window.

"Say, Pete. Have you ever been to the country club?"

"Caddied there summers and bussed tables occasionally on weekends."

"You worked there? Perfect. What should I wear to dinner at the country club?" She tugged at her apron. "I have to confess, I don't know if I'll fit in with country club sorts." She tightened her hands into large fists and shifted on her feet, the rubber soles of her sport shoes squeaked on the wood floor.

Pete had the urge to touch her shoulder. Instead, he shoved his hands in his pockets. He knew the feeling of being out of place. How could he help her? "Depending on the function, dress ranged from formal attire to golf course-casual. But I'd say on a regular dinner night, just wear a simple dress."

She gave Pete a look of relief, warming his heart.

"I've got two possibilities. I'll try them on, and you tell me what you think."

The freckles highlighting her face gave her a childlike quality. He had the urge to kiss her cute nose. *What on earth was he thinking?*

He shrugged.

"I'll be right back."

He and Mister T watched Claudia hurry upstairs, and soon floorboards creaked overhead.

A fashion expert, he was not. Outside, he activated his saw. The power tool shrieked and spewed out sawdust as he made his cuts. He turned to position another board when he saw her.

Claudia stood in the doorway. Her slim figure was accentuated by a simple well-fitted black dress that reached just below the knee. Her hair was pulled back tight and secured. Simple cream-colored pearls graced her ears and neck. Stunning.

She spread her arms and twirled like a model. "My standard black dress. What do you think?"

"Good." Couldn't the brainwave connected to his mouth come up with something better?

Claudia looked lovely, but somehow the little-black-dress-look scrubbed away her individuality. She'd become a country club clone, not bad, just ... not her. He couldn't tell her that. Studying female attire pressed his uneasy button, but at the same time, he appreciated the moment. Pete hoisted cut boards under each arm and tried to think of a more sensible statement.

"That dress should do just fine." He dropped the boards with a clunk onto the back of the tailgate.

"You think so? A black dress can be considered dressy though. I've got another possibility I want you to look at." She disappeared before a response was required.

Amazing how she could change from down-to-earth to sophisticated. And how did he suddenly get the role of fashion critic?

Brushing flecks of sawdust from the freshly cut sheet of birch, he admired the grain. Wood, he could assess. He shook his head, set another sheet of wood on the sawhorses, and measured for his next cuts. He began work on a bracket support when he heard the back door open again.

"How do you like this dress?"

Something inside Pete flip-flopped. Claudia stepped onto the sidewalk, her hair no longer slicked back. Honey-colored curls outlined her face in soft, puffy clouds. She was captivating—breathtaking. His heart hammered, and beads of perspiration dotted his brow. What was wrong with him?

The sleeveless dress of large bright yellow sunflowers on a deep blue background had a simple fitted top with a round neckline and skirt that swayed when she walked. The golden hues in the dress complemented her eyes and hair.

"Well?" she asked, as if she was afraid she had made a ridiculous choice.

Pete swallowed hard and hitched a knot that formed in his throat.

"Uh … uh …" This was nuts. Now he was stuttering.

"I think that dress is … uh … nice." Is *nice* an improvement over *good*?

"Nice," he repeated. His mouth went dry, as if coated with the fine particles of wood laying at his feet. "Very nice. Nothing wrong with wearing that dress at the country club."

"You like this dress better than the black?"

"Yeah," he said shuffling his feet.

His work boots grated over the sand and sawdust on the sidewalk. Was he reverting to being a schoolboy with a crush? He was twenty-eight years old, for heaven's sake.

"Either one is okay."

The "How Much Is that Doggie in the Window" tune sounded. Claudia stepped back and peered through the back door toward the front of her shop. "It's Kali. I can get her opinion too." Claudia disappeared, leaving the back door to the shop open.

Perspiration trickled down Pete's face. It was hot, but he'd be sweating if it were thirty-two degrees. He caught only pieces of conversation but enough to hear Kali wanted her to go with the black dress.

In high school, Kali's friends all dressed alike—pullover shirts in pastel colors and designer jeans or shorts—but they had scattered after graduation. Was Kali trying to shape a new friend into one of her own making? Put her into a mold to suit her purpose? And what was that purpose? Pete kicked at a clump of wood shavings. The puff of dust coated his boots like the hazy concern settling on his heart.

Forget Kali and Claudia. Concentrate on the project at hand.

Chapter 7

The Monday morning sun's rays sifted through the dense oaks in Feldman Park, spotlighting the sparse turf. Pete knocked on the back door of Claudia's shop.

Why the uneasy feeling? He wanted to get started on the restoration of the Hamilton house across the square. And yet, did he honestly want to finish this job?

The dead bolt clicked, the doorknob rattled, and the door swung open. Claudia was dressed in jeans and a T-shirt. Her face looked fresh-scrubbed, with cheeks flushed a bright pink. A headband anchored her curly hair. She looked vibrant and spoke with enthusiasm on the cell phone propped on her shoulder. She motioned Pete to come in, pointed to the phone and whispered, "Elaine. I didn't get to talk to her Sunday."

Pete nodded and returned to his truck to unstrap the bungee cords holding the painted cubicles.

He heard Claudia's chatter behind him. "... so, she apparently tells Mr. Sterling from Birmingham that I'm a dog trainer who will do wonders for his disobedient dog. And this isn't just *any* dog, it's the Cairn terrier whose photo appears on his dog food products. Her introduction put me in an awkward position. You should have seen the look on Kali's face—like, 'please go along with the idea and we'll talk later.' I couldn't help but feel sorry for—" Claudia turned, her eyes widened. "Whoa! Pete. You outdid yourself. Elaine, you've got to come down and see the pink and yellow display cubes Pete built. Okay ... okay, I don't want to hold you up. I'll talk to you later and fill you in on the country club."

After ending her phone call, Claudia clapped her hands like a kid with a new puppy. Her excitement about his work was strange, yet nice.

"How did you get the paint so smooth?" She ran her hand over the surface of the cubicles.

"I have a friend who owns a paint and body shop. He let me use his paint room. Is Elaine busy this morning?"

"She had several customers come in and had to get off the phone. I was telling her about my country club experience. By the way, thanks to Kali, the bistro got another plug in the weekly paper. Did you see the article?" Claudia pointed to the paper on her appointment table.

"I did."

Lyman had titled his write up, *Barkin' Bistro*. Not the most complimentary way to have Elaine's business featured. The stories he spun were marked by attention-grabbing headlines followed by low-quality, little-researched writing, earning him the label, Slyman. At least his work only hit the stands once a week. "Was the information in the article correct? You're a dog trainer, as well as groomer?"

Claudia's smile disappeared. "Kali introduced me that way to the reporter. I ... I used to teach obedience classes. It's been awhile."

Dog obedience training was not a good subject for her. What was Kali up to?

"So, how was your evening at the country club?"

"We had dinner with a businessman from Birmingham, Julius Sterling. Conversation was going fine," Claudia looked down, "until Kali obligated me to train an unruly, celebrity dog belonging to Mr. Sterling. Kali wants to impress him."

Bingo. Kali's objective.

"I've heard of him. He owns a condo on the beach. Is dog obedience training something you intend to offer?"

All her zeal and even a bit of color drained from her face. "I planned to limit my business to grooming and boarding."

Typical Kali. If she had a goal she wanted to attain, she'd engineer circumstances to achieve her objective. Like making a poor schmuck believe she liked him to snag an escort for homecoming queen court.

"Why didn't you tell Kali you wanted to limit your business?"

"Well, I hated to." Claudia flung her expressive hands outward. "Kali must have built me up as some accomplished dog trainer."

"You should have said, 'I have no clue what you're talking about.'"

"I couldn't do that to her." She flopped down on the sofa.

"Do you always let people run over you?"

Claudia wrinkled her forehead. "No. Like Kali said, maybe offering a class will help my business."

"I think you shouldn't let people push you around." He was blunt but didn't want Claudia falling prey to Kali's domination.

"You know what?" Claudia stood and planted her hands on her hips. Sun through the shop window lit up her red hair like fire. "I think we should get off the subject."

"You're right," Pete said and directed his attention to the front window. Of course, she was right. He had no business butting in. But he knew Kali. The idea of her taking advantage of Claudia didn't sit well with him. Heaviness settled in his chest. But what did it matter if Kali's agenda sat well with him or not? What she did, and what Claudia did, was no concern of his.

"Where do you want these cubicles?"

Claudia's entire demeanor changed in an instant. "Hold up. Let me vacuum the carpet in the display window before you set up the cubes."

Pete marveled at how she could turn their conversation-gone-sour to sweet in one breath. An enviable trait. He took a deep breath. She even lightened his spirit.

Pete went back to his truck to unload a green cubicle. He returned just in time to see Claudia vacuuming with her back to him and about to take a spill off the ledge of the display window. He grabbed her as she stepped onto thin air, breaking her fall by hugging her middle with one arm.

The vacuum flew into the air, landed on top of the yellow cube, and clattered to the floor. The rapid beat of his heart thundered in his eardrums with her body pressed against his. She smelled fresh, like the sheets his mother used to hang out in the sun to dry. With her feet touching the floor, he released her abruptly. Contact with her felt entirely too good.

Claudia rushed to exam the cubicle.

"Oh, Pete. There's a big gash in the wood." She looked as if she might cry.

"I can fix scratched wood. It would be harder to fix you. Are you all right?"

"Yes, yes. Thank you. I feel terrible."

"Don't worry." Pete stooped down to inspect the damage. "A little wood filler and paint will take care of the problem."

"You're sweet, but I'm afraid I have to warn you, mishaps seem to happen when I'm around."

"Happens to all of us."

She drew in a sharp breath. "My experience goes way beyond what happens to most."

Pete had managed to strike another awkward subject. The girl turned emotions on and off like a faucet.

She ran her finger over the gash. "I'm so sorry."

Pete shrugged "Really. I can fix it where you won't even know the scratch was there."

Claudia plunked down on the ledge of the display window. "I walked a dog past the Hamilton house yesterday. Looks like you have lots of work ahead, especially if you fit other jobs like mine around the restoration."

"I've taken off some time from the oil rigs, so I'll have uninterrupted time to work."

"Oil rigs?"

Pete nodded. "When I'm not working offshore, remodeling is what I do. I plan to fit small jobs around the Hamilton house project, especially when I'm working for Helping Hands."

"On the oil rigs, you're completely surrounded by water?" Her voice carried a note of alarm.

"Yes."

"Days on end, no land in sight?" Her face went pale.

"There are amazing sunrises and sunsets. The job kind of grows on you after a while."

Claudia shivered, changing the conversation back to restoring old houses. The girl shook off her odd concern like water on a wet dog. He'd never seen anyone who could move from one topic and mood to another as fast as she could.

"Fixing up that old place should be fun."

"Some think I'm crazy."

"Oh, no." She clasped her hands together. "I've always wanted to restore an old house to its original glory, where you could virtually travel back in time and experience what life was like for the former residents." She crossed her sandaled feet at the ankles and wriggled pink painted toenails. "You know what I mean?"

Pete enjoyed her eagerness. "I never really thought about time travel, but exploring construction design and building material from the past is a part of my interest in the place."

Claudia lifted her eyes upward as if trying to see inside her own creative mind. "Can't you just picture a little girl having a tea party with her dolls on the big front porch in days gone by?"

"Not really."

Her vision sent Pete's mind to the rundown playhouse he was supposed to restore. He'd envisioned the house with a wife and his own kids. But the dream had evaporated with a note left on his apartment door—*I go. I marry. Apology.*

Lidia, his one-time fiancée, spoke with broken English, but he got the idea. She'd found another schnook willing to marry her right away and give her legal status. From the night they met, she'd pushed for a wedding. She cooked, cleaned his apartment and clung to his words, working hard to learn English. She seemed devoted and loving, though impatient to set a date. He returned from the oil rigs in early January, ready to make her his bride. But all that was left of her was a note.

Claudia tapped her index finger on her forehead. "Put your imagination to work."

Pete shook his head and smiled. Where would her mind go next?

She pointed at the display. "You know what I picture in the window?" Not waiting for a response, she arranged the open-ended cubes on the platform. "The yellow one can house a small dog for adoption. When the agency sends a big dog, I'll put a large kennel under the pink cube."

"When will you start receiving the dogs from the humane society?"

"A week from today. The public service announcements have already started. I'm excited about the opportunity to help find families for homeless dogs."

"Help the helpless. My dad ingrained that idea into me."

"Is that why you're involved in the Helping Hands Ministry at church?"

"Pretty much. I watched my dad take care of household repairs my grandmother could no longer handle. He made it possible for her to live out her ninety-six years at home."

"Grammas are special, aren't they? I helped start a pet therapy program at my grandmother's nursing home before she passed away."

"How did the therapy work?"

Claudia hesitated before speaking. Not her usual method of operation.

"I asked volunteers to sign up and bring their dogs for a visit. The old folks enjoyed talking to and petting the dogs, and the animals loved the attention. I think I benefitted most by seeing the expressions of the seniors."

"Dogs give unconditional love."

"They do, and seniors have so much to offer, yet are often put aside like strays. What I'd really love to do one day is have a van outfitted for mobile dog grooming combined with a petting service for the elderly." Her passion radiated.

"Several of the senior citizens at The Top would gladly pay for that service." Pete sniffed an acrid odor. "Do you smell something burning?"

"Oh no. The dog biscuits!" Claudia charged upstairs.

She's baking dog biscuits? Pete lowered his head. Claudia was working hard to build her business. He shouldn't criticize her for wanting to help Kali with a dog training request.

In a moment, she returned with a plateful of very brown bone-shaped dog biscuits.

"Try one."

"You're kidding."

"No." She selected one and took a bite. "I always test them before the dogs get them. I have two schnauzers and a poodle coming in later. All my grooming clients get homemade dog treats. I don't want to disappoint them."

She crunched and swallowed. "Not bad." She held one for Pete to try.

Pete gave her a "why-not" shrug and bit into the biscuit.

"What do you think?"

The texture was hard and crumbled into dry crunchy pieces in his mouth. "Tastes kind of like eating a piece of particle board. You must need to be a dog to love these."

"They don't match up to a chocolate chip cookie, but … they are healthy. I make them with whole wheat flour."

"Listen. I owe you an apology."

"You do? For what?" Her emerald eyes leveled on him, making him too self-conscious to maintain eye contact.

"About me saying you let Kali push you around." Pete studied the toes of his work boots an instant, then faced her. "It's not my place to speak to your decision about offering a dog obedience class. And if you want to help Kali and Mr. Sterling out, it's certainly your choice."

Her eyes glinted. "Thank you."

Lesson learned. Why spoil a friendship with Claudia? Check your emotions at the door. From now on, keep your opinions to yourself.

That directive would be easy, if only she didn't manage to unsettle him to his core.

Claudia packaged the cooled dog biscuits and dropped them in the treat basket on the appointment table. Pete went outside. He presented a tough exterior, but she was beginning to see the tender heart underneath.

The shop door opened to its now overly familiar tune. Petite Francine Waterman entered. Dressed in pale blue slacks and matching top, her white hair appeared freshly permed in tight ringlets.

"Hi, Francine, nice to see you."

"Good morning. When I left the beauty shop, I decided to stop by to see you. Looks like you have a work in progress in the front window."

"Pete is building cubicles for the window to showcase the humane shelter's dogs for adoption."

"Pete does good work," Francine said.

Pete entered through the back door.

"We still have a date tonight?" Francine asked Pete and gave Claudia a wink.

"Sure." Pete's expression never changed. He took a new measurement and punched the retractable button on his tape measure. The tape rolled back into place with a *whap*.

"Pete's installing a bathroom light and fan for me."

Pete remained all business. "I'll get your wall unit ready to install and the damaged piece repaired as soon as possible. Francine, I'll see you later." And with that, he picked up the yellow damaged cube and left.

What happened to friendly Pete?

Claudia riffled the edge of the handyman magazine on the table with her thumb.

"I see you're using one of the magazines I donated to the lending library," Francine said.

"Really? The idea for the display cubes came from your magazine." Claudia flipped to the bookmarked page.

Francine compared the picture to the project in the window and gave an approving nod. "I like your interpretation of the idea."

"Did you make this bookmark? I've seen several of them in the donated books."

"I did. These were my husband's magazines. He wouldn't go to church. I thought the Scriptures might be a way to witness to him without nagging."

"Pretty smart."

"I don't know if the bookmarks had anything to do with his change of heart, but he didn't throw them away. He started going to church with me a couple of years before he died." There was a hint of moisture in Francine's eyes.

"How wonderful that you continue to share these bookmarks."

"I hope the Scriptures are an encouragement to people who find them." Francine pulled a tissue from her purse and dabbed at her eyes. "Question for you. My Boston terrier doesn't need a haircut, will you just bathe him for me?"

"Of course."

"I wash Toby in my bathtub, but I have a bad knee, and it's just getting too hard for me to get down and scrub him anymore."

"I would be happy to wash him for you. I just mentioned to Pete that I'd like to have a mobile grooming van one day and provide home service to pet owners like you."

"You'd get enough business at my apartment building to pay for a van in no time."

"I'll keep your vote of confidence in mind." Claudia held up her hand to visually count. "Adopting pets, mobile grooming, then I'd like to provide pet therapy, and now I'm considering … how do you think a dog obedience class would be received here?"

Francine tapped her index finger against her lips. "There might be a market for a class. Many of the dogs at The Top are set in their ways just like their owners. Pets and owners would probably be grateful for a class, especially if it's in walking distance."

Claudia appreciated Francine's readiness to listen. "I haven't worked with dogs for some time. But Kali—you met her at the grand opening?"

"Yes."

"She has a business associate whose dog needs obedience ... tra-training." The word caught in her throat. A cold numbness washed over, and she hugged herself.

The last command she gave to heel ended with her being forced to heel next to a police officer. He escorted her from the Atlanta dog shop where she had worked. Could she put her humiliating trip to jail behind her? Could she revive her skills, and schedule an obedience class? What was she thinking? She couldn't even say the word training without coming undone.

"Since I'm just getting started, I don't want to get in over my head ... but Kali seems to think offering a class might help business."

"If you're having trouble making a decision, have you thought of praying?"

Claudia was taken back a moment. She'd prayed over all kinds of needs with her mom and dad when she was little, and seeking God's direction *was* the topic of her morning devotion. "I hate to say it, but actually no. Praying is exactly what my mom and dad would have suggested."

"Wise parents. Do they live near here?"

Claudia let out a shallow sigh. "Both of my parents passed away in a boating accident when I was nine."

"I'm so sorry. What a terrible thing."

"I was blessed to live with my grandmother until she died. Aunt Lucy took me in, at least until she broke her hip. Then I went into a group home, but I still miss my parents."

"Oh my, what a life you've lived. You *were* blessed to have people who helped you along the way."

Claudia ran her finger over the smooth bookmark. "Writing down Scriptures reminds me of my mom. She used to post them on sticky notes around the house. She wrote a Scripture on the photo taken of them shortly before they died. I wish I had it back."

"What happened to it?"

"During the death investigation, I gave an investigator the picture. It was never returned."

"Do you know what agency worked the case?"

"I'm not sure."

"You should be able to get the photo if the case is closed. Get me the information about the date, location, and agency that worked the accident. I'll check with my friend, Lake. He used to work with my husband in law enforcement and might know someone who could locate the file."

"Thank you. I'll check with Aunt Lucy."

"Now, about your holding a dog obedience class. I'll put the idea on my prayer list. You pray, too, and we'll get back together."

"You'd pray for me about the class?"

"Why, of course." Francine's eyes spoke in earnest. "When should I bring Toby in?"

Claudia checked her appointment book. "How about Monday, around nine?"

"Perfect. And we'll see where prayer leads us. As a matter of fact, let's pray right now."

Francine's hand felt soft and comforting as she grasped Claudia's hand still holding the bookmark.

"Father in heaven, Claudia needs your assistance. She is troubled about a decision to give a dog obedience class and unsure about what to do. You are a God of clarity. We ask your clear direction and thank you in advance for your answer. Amen."

Claudia added an "amen" and felt a tearful tug. Francine's ability to flow into prayer and make conversation with God seemed so natural. It reminded her of sweet moments when she knelt by her bed with her mom and dad for evening prayer.

Francine patted Claudia's hand. "You can trust the Lord to show you the way."

Claudia hugged Francine. Her prayer awakened a place gone dry in Claudia's soul. Could she ever learn to pray that way again?

Chapter 8

Claudia hated being late.

Bless Elaine. She'd saved her a seat. She took a deep breath and forced herself down the center aisle to row "F" where Elaine and Jeff were seated in the old theater, now home to New Hope Community Church.

"Excuse me."

The man in the aisle seat stood for her. Claudia tried to scoot past the lady next to him, but instead lunged sideways, grabbing the man seated in the row in front of her. "Sorry," she whispered, all the while jiggling her foot out of a purse strap. Freeing her foot, she thudded into the seat next to Elaine.

"I am so sorry," Claudia whispered to the lady and straightened her purse. She patted the shoulder of the man she'd grabbed.

If only she had some vanishing cream. People looking at her were going to miss the announcement on the overhead screen about nursery volunteers being needed.

And there was Pete on the front row. Were the corners of his mouth lifted? Yep, that passed for a grin. Claudia positioned the church bulletin to cover her face. Oh, fine. Apparently, all she needed to break through his armor was a bout of clumsiness.

Elaine gave Claudia a sympathetic smile. "Glad you're here."

"There's a story behind my being late." Praise and worship started, making her explanation easier.

"What happened?"

"I was walking my sixty-five-pound Weimaraner boarder, King. I tripped on a tree root, landed in a puddle, and spattered mud all over him. We both had to bathe."

"Could only happen to—oops."

"Might as well say it—my black cloud continues to manifest."

"But you arrived at church successfully. Being late doesn't matter." Music from the band in the old orchestra pit filled the air. Elaine gave Claudia a thumbs-up. They both joined in clapping their hands and singing.

As she sang, troubles slipped away, and the joy of being a child of God filled her heart. The pastor referenced Psalm 37, then began his message.

Claudia stared at the words in the pew Bible. But her thoughts drifted to the grooming shop, the first pet of the week, the new display project … and Pete.

He sat on the front row near the exit. The location, remote and readily accessible for a quick retreat, suited him. Interaction with him yesterday had gone from disagreeable to talkative to apologetic to withdrawn by the time he left. That man had another layer to him. Could she uncover it?

"… and he will give you the desires of your heart."

Claudia tuned into the preacher, who now walked about the stage.

"Sometimes I'm afraid we skip the part about delighting, trusting, committing, and expect God to give us our desires anyway. I've learned that as we delight in him, he might just change our desires to line up with his."

Was offering a dog obedience class the desire of her heart? She'd prayed, and Francine had prayed, but no clear answer had come—only more questions.

Could she teach an obedience class when she couldn't even walk a dog without having to change clothes? What if she lost control of the class? Kali might look bad if she backed out.

Everyone stood. The music team sang softly. Claudia closed her eyes. If she were standing between her parents, long ago, her dad would have put his arm around her, and her mom would have taken her hand. She'd felt safe, loved. Tears pooled in Claudia's eyes.

After the benediction, Claudia followed Elaine and Jeff out of the auditorium into the noisy lobby where her friends left to get their girls.

"Hi, neighbor." Dave Burbank approached with Pete. Francine was right behind them.

"I was just telling Dave about your dream of a van for pet therapy and mobile grooming," Pete said.

"I like the idea. Whenever you're ready, we'd love to have you work with our Helping Hands Ministry. If you offered a dog training class, too, you'd really have a hit."

Claudia looked at Francine and then Pete.

Pete's shrug said Dave didn't hear about her teaching a class from him. With a tilt of Francine's head, Francine sent Claudia a knowing smile.

"I've been approached about an obedience class, but it's been a while since I've trained dogs."

"I bet teaching dog obedience is like riding a bike. I'll let you practice on my Charlie and me."

Pete seemed to be looking for an opening and spoke up. "I have a few Helping Hands projects that need attention the first of the week, but I should be back on your project by Thursday or Friday." He hesitated a second and added, "If that's okay?"

"Of course, whatever works for you."

He nodded. "Dave, I'll see you at the meeting." He left with a swift stride.

"Tell them I'll be right there," Dave called after him.

"I don't want to hold you from your meeting, but … are you serious about a market for an obedience class?" Claudia asked.

"You start it, and they'll come. I know a Boston terrier who could stand some training." Dave rolled his eyes in Francine's direction. "Spoiled, you know." His voice feigned whispering.

"Like Charlie isn't?" Francine nudged Dave with her elbow. "Actually, I'm sure we could both benefit."

Dave snapped his fingers. "Say, why not teach a class at The Top? Several residents own pets. They'd jump at the chance to have a class offered there."

"Who would I have to talk to?"

"Our building manager, Mr. Markham. I'll talk to him and call you later." He glanced at his watch. "I'd better get to my meeting."

Francine gently patted Claudia on her shoulder. "I think our prayers for direction about the class have just received an open door."

"Do you really think so?"

"We'll know if you get an okay from our building manager."

Claudia took in a deep breath and smiled. "Oh." She opened her purse. "I got the information about my parents' case from Aunt Lucy." Claudia handed Francine a paper.

"Good. I'll ask Lake to see what he can do about obtaining that photo."

Francine waved at a couple of ladies going to the fellowship hall. "I have to help set up for a little luncheon with my Sunday school class. We bring a covered dish whenever there's something to celebrate. Won't you join us? We always have plenty."

Claudia didn't want to go empty-handed, but she had no other lunch plans. "I appreciate the invitation. What are you celebrating?"

"Would you believe, National Anti-Boredom Month?"

For Claudia, boredom was hardly an issue, especially if she ventured into dog training—the very thing she'd vowed never to do again.

Thwak. Pete unhooked one of the bungee cords holding Claudia's project in the back of his truck parked behind The Pampered Pooch.

"Good heel." Through the morning haze hanging over Feldman Park, Claudia came into view with a little dog walking at her side. She waved and picked up her pace. The multi-color dog trotted along in sync.

Claudia's unruly ponytail splayed like fireworks. And not just her hair—everything about her commanded his attention. *She's a client, Cullen.*

"Good morning." Claudia's eyes sparkled.

Her effervescent grin hit Pete with a jolt to the heart. There was no way he was making eye contact. He nodded and held up the yellow cubical.

"You fixed the piece I messed up?" She ran her hand over the repair. "You work miracles." Her words came out breathless, and he thought she might tear up.

"Not hardly. Just wood putty and paint."

"How did your Helping Hands work go?"

"Fine. Dave and I fixed a leaky roof and built a wheelchair ramp."

"You're wonderful to give your time for those projects. Activity here at the shop has picked up. We have catching up to do."

There she went, switching topics and encircling him with her inclusion talk like they were longtime friends. She was good at it. "We do?" He had to admit he missed seeing her the past few days.

Claudia gave a decisive nod and held up the dog leash. The small, short-haired, brown and white dog crouched as if ready to jump up. "Sit." The dog sat at her side.

"Who's this little guy?"

The dog perked up his ears.

"Meet Clover, my first pet of the week. Isn't he adorable? I've decided to adopt him."

"Good for you and him." Pete stooped down. "Hey, boy." Clover wagged his long, skinny tail.

"He's a stray. Not sure how old he is, maybe a year. I named him Clover because ... look at this." She pointed to the dog's hindquarters which sported an odd brown spot. "Kali saw the clover shape and suggested the name."

Pete studied the pattern and squinted his eyes, trying to make a clover pattern materialize. "I'd say the splotch looks more like a heart."

"Hmm ... I don't know."

Clover put his front paws on Pete's leg.

Pete set the yellow display piece by the door, picked up Claudia's adoptee, and scratched the dog behind the ears. The frisky guy worked his way to Pete's face and licked his chin.

"I think he likes you."

Pete wiped at the dog's moist affection with the back of his hand. "You're pretty likeable yourself, boy." Pete gave Clover a few more pats before setting him down.

Claudia continued to talk nonstop.

"Dave set things up for me to do a trial dog obedience class at The Top of the Harbor. Eight have signed up already. Kali's been a tremendous help."

Unless she'd done a one-eighty, Kali didn't do things out of the kindness of her heart.

"How is Kali helping?"

"By going through a maze of boxes in storage to find my old dog training manuals. I've been working on the basics with Clover. Kali wants to learn the commands."

Somehow, he couldn't picture Kali putting herself out to work with a dog. But who knows? Maybe she'd changed. Unlikely, but maybe.

"The class next week will be a practice class for me. Kali hopes to learn commands with Clover, then impress Mr. Sterling when he takes the class later. She said the four-leaf clover is a sign he'll bring her good luck."

Ah. The ulterior motive. "Shouldn't Kali be the one working him?"

"She's in Birmingham and will be back later today. Did you know she's afraid of dogs? She had a bad experience with a dog as a child and had to get stitches on her arm. I'm teaching Clover the basic commands so Kali will have an easier time working with him. I tell you, studying my skills manuals, I feel like I'm back in college cramming for finals."

Claudia knelt and stroked Clover. "You'll make Kali look like a pro, won't you boy?"

Kali was using Claudia, and she didn't have a clue. He watched her petting Clover. She was like a cute, bright-eyed, irresistible puppy herself. He didn't want to see her hurt.

"I'd make sure she puts in the time with Clover and not leave all the work to you."

"Oh, I don't mind."

Claudia's people-pleasing nature was admirable but just the type Kali would target. He'd better let it go. The tailgate dropped with a thud. No need to instigate another disagreement.

Claudia gestured across the park. "I walk Clover by the Hamilton house every day. When will you start restoration?"

"Soon as I finish your project." He walked around his truck and began undoing the cords holding additional project pieces under protective blankets.

"You must be excited about working on the house … that is, if you get excited about anything."

Pete arched an eyebrow and cut a look in her direction.

She turned the intensity of her green eyes on him. "No offense. You seem to be an even-keeled guy. Level-headed. Don't let things bother or excite you. Am I right?"

"Maybe."

She must think him a terrible bore.

"Help me uncover these cubes, and I'll set them up."

"Sure." Claudia held one corner, and they pulled back the quilted covering exposing cubicles painted in colors of fresh lime, hot pink, and bright yellow. Some of the display pieces sported patterns of polka dots, and stripes.

"Oh, Pete." Claudia 's eyes widened.

She either hated or really liked the results.

"These are beautiful." She touched the painted surface of one. "How did you … When did you? I thought you were busy with Helping Hands projects."

"Afternoons and evenings."

"Amazing." Claudia scooted around both sides of the truck like an eager child on Christmas morning, then spread her arms in an arching motion as if pronouncing a blessing and said, "They are magnificent."

She spoke with such spirit. What could he say? "Thanks."

Claudia turned to Pete. "I have an idea. Could you show me how to build a display cube from leftover scraps?"

Another surprise from the girl with a red ringlet escaping from her headband. How would touching her cheek and brushing the stray strand in place feel?

Focus Cullen. An answer. Give her an answer.

"I ... uh, suppose."

"Could I really learn?"

"I don't know why not. I'll install the wall shelf for the small kennels first, and we'll see what kind of materials we have left."

"Can I help with the wall shelf too? I don't have any grooming appointments scheduled."

Pete preferred to work alone. "Uh ... I ..."

"Fantastic."

She apparently took his stutter as a "yes."

She unlocked her back door and said, "Clover, into the window while we glamorize the shop."

Pete followed her, carrying two of the project pieces. The rich aroma of cooking food permeated the shop.

"Something smells good," Pete said.

"Pot roast in my slow cooker. Kali's coming for dinner tonight."

"Smells like she's in for a treat."

"My aunt gave me the recipe." She put Clover in his kennel under the lime green cubicle in the display window. "There you go, buddy. Remember, don't look too cute today," she cautioned with a pointed index finger. "You are spoken for."

The shop phone rang. Claudia stumbled on nothing in particular but recovered quickly and answered. "Pampered Pooch. I love 'em while I suds 'em."

Pete snickered as he returned to his truck. Claudia lifted his spirits, but a concern nagged at him.

Would Kali's agenda change Claudia's spirit?

Chapter 9

Claudia hung up the phone and penciled Appleberry into the one o'clock slot in her appointment book. Humming the "doggie in the window" theme, she patted O'Flannery's little leprechaun hat and headed outside to join Pete.

"Corky and Fritz are up to their old tricks."

"How so?"

"They chased a bird and fell into a fishpond. Olivia requested an emergency grooming job at one. So, I'm available as your handyman for the morning—or should I say handywoman?"

Pete shrugged his shoulders and pulled a long shelf painted hot pink from the truck bed. "Those bichons need your obedience class."

Claudia shuddered. "The brothers might give me more of a teaching challenge than I'm prepared for right now." She rubbed her hands together. "Where do we start?"

"Installing the shelf and trim for the small kennels."

Inside the shop, Claudia handed screws to Pete while he secured brackets and hung the shelf. Pete said little. If there was to be any conversation, she'd have to take the initiative.

"Your craftiness is going to make my shop look great. Where does the trim go?"

"Against the shelf edge. Hold the trim in place while I attach it."

"Do you use glue?"

"No, nails."

Nails. A topic for discussion. "What kind of nails?"

He shook some nails into his hand from a plastic container and held them for Claudia to inspect. "These are finishing nails. The small head helps conceal the nail."

"Neat. Nothing like a little nail knowledge."

Claudia held the trim in place and watched Pete work. His closeness made her ultra-aware of his clean soap scent. He might come across as brusque, but his plain-spoken manner and unpretentious ways gave her a sense of … sense of what? Stability? Security? Whatever the label, she liked those simple, natural qualities in him.

"I brought some yellow and green paint in case you wanted to add a design on the trim."

At last, an unsolicited remark. "I know the perfect thing." Claudia hurried to the dog-lover magazines stacked on the floor by the love seat and shuffled through them. "Here." She produced a page with a series of paw prints. "How would this design look?"

"Fine. I'll get some trim scraps from the truck for practice."

Claudia focused on Pete as he walked out the back door of the shop. Clover's kennel rattled. He strained to see down the back hall.

"You're captivated by him, too, aren't you?"

Clover wagged his tail. Claudia spotted O'Flannery eying them both. "Okay, okay. I admit," she whispered, "I find him … attractive."

Pete returned with pieces of trim and a box of painting supplies. What would he think if he knew she'd just shared a confidence about him with a ceramic statue?

He removed the paint can lids. "These are open paint cans. Remember where they are." She caught the glint in his eye, as he tilted his head in her direction.

"Don't worry. Polyurethane oozing onto Elaine's floor is etched permanently on my brain." She thrust her hands on her hips and bumped the nail container with her elbow, scattering finishing nails all over the floor.

"Oh great."

"At least they don't ooze."

Another unsolicited remark. Claudia dropped to the floor and began gathering. Why, oh why did these accidents happen to her? With no further comment, Pete helped collect the nails, secured the container lid, and handed her a small brush.

"You think you can trust me with a paint brush?"

"Therein lies the reason for practice trim. Give it a try. You'll do fine."

Claudia's wounded spirit lifted with his encouragement. Pete was a natural at reproducing the paw prints. Claudia had to work at perfecting the technique a little longer. She studied the paw print sample closely. "If I draw a Hershey's kiss with four jellybeans on top …" Claudia pressed her lips together and concentrated on her strokes with the green paint. "What do you think?" She held up her latest attempt for Pete to critique.

"Looks good. Let's start at the center and work to the ends."

"Can we alternate the colors?"

"We can exchange brushes as we work."

The shop was quiet, and the continual nearness when they swapped brushes, made the tiny hairs on her arms stand at attention. Her heartbeat accelerated with each paintbrush exchange. Could he hear the pounding of her heart? Although she found Pete hard to read, his reserve intrigued her. When he occasionally made eye contact, she wanted to know everything about him—his history, his thoughts, his opinions. He, however, seemed totally oblivious to her presence, so she tried to concentrate on creating paw prints.

"Done with my side. How about you, Pete?"

"Just finishing."

"Let's step back and examine our creation."

Pete stood beside her to observe their handiwork. Clover peered out of the kennel.

"We did good, huh, Clover?"

Clover returned one sharp bark.

Claudia met Pete's hand in an overhead high-five. Wow. Their touch created a zap of tingles like the time she touched a light switch while standing on wet concrete. Finally, he flashed a wide smile revealing deep dimples in his cheeks. Double wow. That awesome smile was worth the wait.

Behind the grooming shop, Pete handed Claudia the electric circular saw, and her face lost all color. He'd placed a sheet of wood on the sawhorses. Claudia was about to get her first lesson in basic carpentry.

Acutely aware of her arm touching his, Pete attempted to focus on identifying the saw parts.

"Here are the blade guards, motor housing, cutting depth adjustment knob, the safety, and the trigger switch."

"Seriously? You trust me with a skill saw?"

"Absolutely. Put these on." He handed her a pair of safety glasses. "There's nothing like grinding through a piece of wood with a power-driven saw blade to test your luck."

She gave him a leery look. "Yeah, well ... there's an old saying. You shouldn't push your luck."

Was the hovering black cloud conversation he'd overheard at the bistro with Elaine what bothered her? Although unsure why, he wanted to help her see herself in a more positive light. "Thinking you're destined to mess up is no way to approach handling a power tool. What matters is learning proper technique, safety measures, and how to apply them."

"Like training a dog?" her voice small.

"I suppose so. Align the saw's blade with the line I drew and hold the saw steady. Don't push too hard. Let the saw do the work. You just guide."

Claudia hesitated. "If I want a side table for my magazines, I guess I have to try, don't I?"

"Yup." Pete kept his focus on the saw blade. Claudia finally pressed the trigger. The saw squealed. The blade spun. Claudia pushed the grinding wheel forward, carefully following the line Pete had drawn, and made a perfect cut.

She let out her breath and yelped. "I did it! You've no idea the risk you were taking by standing next to me with a power saw."

"Sound instruction can turn inept into capable." Pete was on a roll and added abruptly, "But if you continue to berate and label what you do, you'll be stuck acting as if you're a klutz."

Claudia bit her lower lip.

Had he been too harsh? He moved on. "There are a lot of different ways to construct joints."

"You think I'm acting?"

Was she going to cry? Tough jobs and physical work he could handle. But tears?

"I didn't say ... Sorry, I was out of line."

"No." She held her hand up. "People are entitled to their own opinions." Her eyes held his for a moment.

His chest felt heavy. Why didn't he keep his opinions to himself as he usually did? Why change now? With her?

"You were talking about joints?"

Amazing how she did that—taking criticism in stride and moving past his blunt remark.

"Yes, uh … I'll show you just one of many ways to join wood pieces. I used one-quarter-inch plywood to make the cubes light enough to move easily. So, a frame is needed for strong corners." Pete pulled long pieces of wood from the back of the truck. "These are one-by-two-inch wood strips to cut and form the frame. The plywood will attach to the frame."

"Okay." Claudia pursed her lips and listened attentively.

Pete marked the wood strips, and Claudia made the cuts.

"Super handywoman." Claudia grinned.

He enjoyed working with her. Surprising. "You're doing great. Now put on wood glue."

He demonstrated how much glue to use and handed the tube to her.

"Got it," she said. Pete was amused to see her tongue-poked-in-cheek concentration.

"Next, it's all attached with casing nails."

"A new kind of nail?"

She really seemed enthused. "This nail has a slim shank, cone shaped top, and is used to fasten lighter types of wood."

Claudia hammered in the last nail and handed him the hammer. Her hair held the light fragrance of jasmine and tugged at his senses.

Their eyes met, and he had the strong urge to kiss her. *Great.*

He gave the last nail a final whap. *He needed to finish this job.*

Claudia lifted their table creation. "To think, this little table materialized from a flat piece of wood."

They were friends who appreciated the creative process. That's it. Put a lid on it. Pick up the tools and leave. No more eye contact. Be professional. All he had to do was stay clear of her delicately scented mass of red curls, and he wouldn't get hurt.

She set their project on the tailgate and faced Pete. "Thank you for trusting me with a power tool."

His heart connected with her sincerity. He wanted to affirm her. Hold her.

He slapped his hand on the table and blurted, "What color would you like me to paint this project?"

"I don't want you going to more trouble. I'll paint it."

"No trouble. Pick a color."

Claudia gave him a glimpse of her emerald eyes. "How about green?"

"Green it is."

"It's almost noon," Claudia said, glancing at her watch. "I can fix peanut butter and jelly sandwiches for us while I check the roast."

Declining her offer would get him out of there. Now would be the perfect time to be on his way. Pete's stomach rumbled. But what's the harm in staying for PB&J? *Don't do it.*

"Sounds good."

"Creamy or crunchy?" Claudia leveled her eyes on his as if the question was serious business.

"Crunchy."

Claudia let out a triumphant, "Yes," and connected her hand with Pete's for another high-five.

When she left for the kitchen, he put the tools and supplies in the truck's toolbox and retrieved his broom and dustpan. As he swept up the sawdust and wood trimmings, he repeated "just friends" with each stroke of the broom. He could work and enjoy her company as an associate. Right?

If only he could convince his erratic heart.

Chapter 10

"I used an electric saw and didn't hurt anything." Claudia announced to Clover.

His ears at attention, he banged his tail against the bars of his kennel in the shop window.

"And now I'm off to use a knife to spread peanut butter."

Claudia trotted upstairs. Pete had entrusted her with a saw. She still couldn't believe it. He might be distant and outspoken at times but working with him was fun.

She checked the slow cooker. The aroma of the simmering pot roast filled the air and was probably driving poor Clover crazy. She set aside some meat for Clover and added potatoes and carrots that were peeled and chopped earlier. Then she gathered sandwich makings and started spreading crunchy peanut butter on bread.

The shop phone extension rang. She answered and put the phone on speaker.

"Hey, girlfriend."

"Kali, hi." Before Kali could say anything, Claudia told her all she and Pete had accomplished during the morning. "When did you get back?"

"I didn't make it back."

"You're still in Birmingham?"

"Right. Mr. Sterling gave me a desk to use in his office complex, and I'm having to stay longer than I planned. I hate to cancel dinner with you, but—"

"No apologies. Your own desk? Sounds like you're getting your foot in the door—big time."

"I hope so. Let's get together tomorrow night. My treat."

"Why not do leftovers? I'll just reheat the roast. There is way too much for just me."

"Is Pete still there?"

"Yes. I happen to be making peanut butter and jelly sandwiches for our lunch. Another gourmet meal you're missing."

"Yum. If it's creamy peanut butter, I wish I was there."

"Nope. Pete and I are crunchy PB&J connoisseurs."

"Why not ask Pete to stand in for me tonight? I don't want your efforts to go to waste."

"Good idea. I'll ask him." Claudia finished spreading the jelly over the peanut butter, put bread on top and began to slice one diagonally.

"I've got more good news. Mr. Sterling is taking vacation time at his Hamilton Harbor condo and plans to attend all six sessions of your obedience course."

Claudia dropped the knife. "But this is my practice class." She jerked her foot out of the way before the knife fell from the counter and hit the floor. "He lives in Birmingham. I still don't understand why he doesn't get his dog trained there."

"He's tried two different classes here. Says he needs to get out of Birmingham for uninterrupted time to devote to Bitsy."

"Kali, operating a power tool is one thing, but I'm not ready for somebody like Sterling."

"Nonsense."

"I want to do a good job to help you, but what happens if I botch things?"

"Don't worry. I'll be there for moral support."

"Do you still want that horseshoe? You may need it for luck."

"No need when I've got you for good luck."

"Seriously? I've been considered a lot of things but never good luck."

"Is Clover ready to help me impress Mr. Sterling?"

"He's coming along, but—"

"No buts. You'll do great. Now, wish me good fortune on a special deal I'm putting together."

Claudia finished cutting the sandwiches. "You have my good wishes." She looked at her Bible on the kitchen table. "And I'll add you to my prayer list."

"Fantastic. Now remember, it's girls' night out for dinner tomorrow. I have a special place in mind that you're gonna love. Tell Pete to eat an extra portion for me."

"Will do ... if he decides to have dinner with me."

"I have a feeling he will."

Claudia hung up and hurried downstairs with their lunch.

Outside, Pete had finished cleaning the work area.

"Slight change in plans for tonight."

"Oh?"

"Kali is still in Birmingham. She hates missing my pot roast but suggested I invite you and not let the dinner go to waste. Have you got any plans tonight?"

Pete scrutinized Claudia. "You're only asking me because of Kali's suggestion?"

"Well ... not entirely." She felt her face warming. "I would like you to join me too."

Pete offered a quirky smile, "In that case, I accept. Besides, after smelling your roast all day, I feel like an old hound dog hoping he'll get a bite."

She lifted the paper sack. "PB&J to hold us over."

"Good, but first I want to see if the shelf trim is dry and set up the small kennels."

Claudia helped as Pete arranged the kennels inside the colorful cubicles.

"It works," Pete said, inspecting the finished wall unit.

Claudia nudged Pete with her elbow. "Works? It's awesome. Isn't it, Clover?"

Clover's full-bodied wag jiggled his cage.

"You've been a good boy. You deserve a break."

When Claudia released Clover from the kennel, the dog leaped off the platform and ran straight for Pete.

"Look. Clover is taken by you."

Pete bent down to give Clover some special attention. "The feeling is mutual, boy."

Claudia's suspicions were confirmed. Beneath Pete's rough, sometimes disagreeable, exterior lay a kind interior. And Clover knew it too.

Scared. No other word could define the tremors racing over his senses.

Pete had showered and changed into a sport shirt and khakis. He'd splashed on cologne Lidia had given him, then grabbed a washcloth and attempted to scrub the smell off, leaving his skin red and irritated. He'd poured the remaining cologne in the toilet and flushed. If he could only do the same with the memories of the pale-faced woman with haunting gray eyes that had drawn him to her. He thought the Czech woman had joined with him in a unified purpose to build a new life as she adjusted to a new country. The latter turned out to be true, but Lidia decided he wasn't the guy she wanted.

Now standing at Claudia's back door, the cologne scent, though faint, lingered and poked at his self-confidence.

He placed a bottle of sparkling juice on the sidewalk, so he could wipe his sweaty palms on his slacks. He raised his hand to knock then pulled it back.

This was nuts. He was here for dinner with a friend. Not a date. It just felt like a date. He raised his hand again, made a fist, and finally knocked on the door.

The streetlight outlined ungainly, moss-draped oak limbs reaching out from Feldman Park. A slight wind off the bay nudged the trees, creating eerie shadows that creeped back and forth along the street's edge. The evening breeze carried the smell of the pot roast from Claudia's upper apartment and stirred his appetite. He was a stand-in for a home-cooked meal. How hard could playing substitute be?

The bolt lock clinked. He retrieved the bottle of juice as Claudia opened the door.

She wore white slacks and a light pink sleeveless top that added softness to her face. Her hair was tamed into shoulder-length tendrils. Striking.

"You need better lighting back here." Safe subject. "Might want to call the power company and have a dusk to dawn light added." Stick to practicalities. Don't stutter.

"Good idea. I probably should have more light added." Claudia stepped aside and opened the door wider. "Well…?"

"Well, what?"

"Well, come in. You've been in and out all day. Don't feel like you need an invitation now."

"Yeah, um …" Pete stepped in, and Claudia closed the door behind him.

"I didn't know if you drank wine, so I brought some sparkling juice." He placed the bottle in Claudia's hands.

"How sweet. Thank you." She flashed him a smile. "Come upstairs. Everything's ready except the rolls. They'll only take a few minutes."

Pete climbed the stairs behind Claudia. He studied the wooden staircase that creaked underfoot and smelled of lemon oil. The craftsmanship was simple, using beautifully grained wood.

"Do you know how old this building is?"

"Margaret, the lady I bought the shop from, said the building was constructed in 1920."

"These stairs are well built—good, solid wood."

"For me, the stairs were a selling point." They reached the landing at the top of the stairs. "Here's my little abode. It could use some decorating ideas from Izzie and your refurbishing skills, but that will have to wait for another day. Right now, the apartment is comfortable, and I have a great view of Main Street."

In front of him was a living area, to the right, kitchen and dining. The simple oak table was set with candles, navy placemats, and cream-colored plates.

"Have a seat," she said, motioning Pete to the couch in the living room. "I'll get some glasses for the sparkling juice. Hope you don't mind Mason jars."

"Mason jars were my family's regular drinking glasses."

Pete took a seat on the overstuffed beige couch. A dog obedience training manual lay open on the coffee table.

"I have a question for you."

"Shoot," Claudia said as she handed him a glass. She sat in the chair opposite him.

"You said you used to train dogs. Why did you quit?"

Claudia pressed her lips together, her friendly countenance changed. Pete immediately wanted to retract the question. "I'm sorry. I shouldn't meddle."

"No, no. It's just … well, I taught classes that became a … uh … center of controversy. An apparent knack I have. And I didn't want to take on too much—being a new owner, redecorating, establishing a grooming clientele and all."

"Why not tell Kali?"

Claudia scrunched her nose. "I want to help her. She's made me feel so welcome here."

Pete listened and gave a quick nod. What did it matter if Kali did have her own agenda? He'd best not comment further. He got up to take a closer look at a wall hanging.

"Interesting, don't you think?" Claudia said.

The frame held yellowed paper with blue printing that looked like … not only looked like but *was* an exact copy of the paper Marigold showed him when they discussed finding the secret room.

"Where did you get this?"

"Mellie, Margaret's sister who used to own the Flower Cottage behind me, said the paper was discovered in a vault in the apartment over the shop."

Pete lifted a brow. "Really? And she gave the drawing to you?"

"No, no. I'm storing Margaret's belongings in my attic while she travels. I left this picture hanging because it's interesting. Looks like a treasure map, don't you think?" Claudia pressed in close and pointed to a spot on the drawing. "See the X?"

"The drawing …" How much should he say? The closer she got, the harder it was to think. "… reminds me of documents the Hamilton sisters shared with me."

"Really? Were all the houses on the square built at the same time?"

"No, but the original occupants of the houses were connected."

"So, if this mysterious *X* has something to do with Feldman Square, we could be walking right by the *X*, whatever the *X* is, every day and not know it?"

Her attention was focused on the drawing, but her nearness yanked at his nerve endings. Pete returned to the safety of his seat. "Could be. We probably often miss seeing something in plain sight when our surroundings become routine."

"Corky and Fritz both approve of the kennel covers you made."

Her first topic change. Pete took a sip of the sparkling grape juice to keep from smiling. The bubbles tickled his throat—refreshing—like Claudia with her upbeat, changeable personality. "What makes you think they approve?"

"Those two are usually excitable and bark at the passersby or anything that moves. They were quiet and peaceful today. I think the cubicles make them feel cozy and protected."

"The covers probably prevent distractions, like blinders on a horse."

"You should apply for a patent and sell your design to dog groomers across the nation." She held up her glass in a toast.

Pete smiled. "You have big dreams." He looked into his glass and watched the bubbles rising.

"I know. And I wonder if dreaming is a good or bad trait." The oven timer sounded. "The rolls. Bring your glass and pour us a refill."

Claudia placed the pot roast and vegetables in serving dishes, removed steamed broccoli from the microwave, and pulled a tossed green salad from the refrigerator. "Pete, light the candles and pour us some water too, please. The lighter is on the counter and the glasses are on the table."

When everything was ready, they sat down.

"Mind if I pray?" Pete asked.

"Uh ... oh, are you worried?" Her eyebrows drew together.

A heat hit Pete's face and spread to his ears. "No ... I didn't mean—"

"Lighten up. I'm kidding." She grinned, her face radiant in the candlelight.

He relaxed. "It's just ... I'm accustomed to praying before a meal."

"Please. Go ahead."

Claudia bowed her head. Pete prayed a brief blessing over the food and tacked on a silent request that his bad track record with female relationships wouldn't hurt their friendship.

Chapter 11

Claudia blinked back the moisture in her eyes and glanced at Pete across the table. She was thankful he'd come to dinner. Her father had prayed before meals. Unlike many of her childhood friends' families, her family used to eat dinner together. That tradition instilled a sense of security she didn't recognize at the time but longed for when it was lost.

"Thank you for praying." Claudia passed the pot roast to Pete. "Tell me about the Hamilton sisters."

"Marigold and Petunia?"

"That's their names?"

Pete graced her with a grin. Oh, those grand, deep-chiseled dimples.

"That's how the paperwork reads, and they are complete opposites. Marigold is tall, stern, and in charge. Petunia is short, rather submissive with a stubborn streak, but follows her sister's lead." Pete served his plate and handed the dish back to Claudia. "The two explained some of the history of the house and the neighborhood."

"Tell me. Old homes and history fascinate me." She scooted the salad bowl in his direction. "Let's handle service family style."

Pete helped himself to salad. Claudia was relieved to see Pete relax as he shared his story.

"The Hamilton home was built in 1912 for Truman and Rosalyn Hamilton. They had two children—a boy, Gardner, and girl, Regina. Gardner was Rosalyn's maiden name."

"So, where do these girls fit in?"

"Truman and Rosalyn were their grandparents. But the family relationships get interesting." Pete paused to drink some water.

"Truman Hamilton was the owner of a shipping company that operated out of the harbor at the end of Main Street. The house next door to the Hamilton's belonged to Albert and Edith Feldman."

"As in Feldman Park?"

"One in the same. Albert Feldman owned and managed a sawmill situated on the bay, east of the harbor. Their businesses were dependent on each other, with Feldman using Hamilton's company to ship his lumber. The Feldmans also had two children, a boy and a girl."

"So, who were the flower girls' parents?"

"Let me see if I can explain with a diagram." Pete pulled a pen from his pocket and spread out his paper napkin.

Claudia moved the serving dishes to give him more space.

"Here is Feldman Park." He drew a large square. "On this side is the town, one street over from Main. Your shop would be about here." Pete penned in The Pampered Pooch, then the six houses on the square, and labeled the owners.

Claudia was not only fascinated to see the square materialize on the napkin but the spark in Pete's eyes as he talked.

"The Hamiltons and Feldmans gave their children a special gift when they turned twenty-one—a house."

"A house as a birthday gift? I'd say that *was* special."

"Now, here's the kicker. In 1937, the Hamilton and Feldman children all got married."

"All of them? Four weddings in one year must have been the talk of the town."

"I would imagine, except there were only two weddings. The Hamilton children hooked up with the Feldman children." Pete drew arrows. "Edgar Feldman married Regina Hamilton, they had two boys, Harry and Reuben. Gardner Hamilton married Violet Feldman and they had two girls—"

"Marigold and Petunia?"

Pete nodded.

"What a great story. The mom and girls are the flowers, and the dad is the gardener. Who lived in the other two houses?"

"There's more intrigue with World War I involved but one home was a private school, which later became the home of Edgar and Regina. The Feldmans built a duplicate of their house for Violet. But when she and Gardner married, her house became the town's first garden club. Regina's house is now The Flower Cottage and the only one still occupied. The other five eventually became rentals and are now empty."

"Wouldn't restoring all the homes on the square be grand?"

"I'd love to take on the challenge, but I'll have to see how the Hamilton house restoration goes first." Pete put his pen in his pocket and started to crumple the napkin.

Claudia put her hand on his to stop him.

"No, don't mess up your drawing, I want to keep it." She became acutely aware of the warmth of his hand underneath hers. The blue of his eyes deepened when their eyes met.

"You really want to keep my scribbling?"

"I do." She removed her hand. Did he notice that touching him was affecting her? "Your drawing will help me keep the history around here straight."

Pete turned his hand over and released the rumpled napkin. Smoothing it, Claudia placed the napkin on the end of her kitchen counter.

"Ready for coffee and dessert? I made an easy frozen parfait of ice cream and pudding."

"I'm ready."

Pete helped Claudia clear and put the dessert and coffee on the table.

Taking a bite of the creamy mixture, Claudia pointed her empty parfait spoon at Pete. "How did Marigold and Petunia end up with all the houses?"

"I don't know the whole history, but I'm guessing everyone else died leaving the girls sole heirs."

"It's a shame they've let the houses run down."

Pete gave a decisive nod. "When the shipping industry moved from the downtown harbor to the deep-water port, Marigold and Petunia decided to move too. That's when the houses became rentals. Eventually the upkeep and repairs were costing more than the rent, so the houses were closed."

"It seems like they would have sold them rather than let them deteriorate."

"The sisters have a vision to help rebuild the downtown area. They obtained a historical restoration loan which will pay for materials and labor. And if my restoration meets their requirements, they will sell me the house at the fair market price and give me a contract to restore the next house."

"Either way, the house gets restored, and you may or may not end up the owner?"

"Those are the terms of the agreement."

Claudia freshened their coffee. "That seems risky for you."

Pete paused as soft lines creased his brow. "I feel confident I can meet their specifications. If the Feldman Park houses are restored and sold to families, revitalization of the city will be helped, and the historical district downtown expanded."

"With my shop right in the middle. I like that idea."

"Maybe I can get the sisters to require each family own at least one pet that needs grooming." Pete spoke with a straight-faced expression but a twinkle in his eye. Delightful.

"Now you're talkin'."

They finished their desserts. Cleanup was shared—Pete washed dishes while Claudia dried and put away. The activity, at first awkward, became comfortable, just as working alongside him had been earlier in the day.

Pete stared at the coffee pot.

"More coffee?"

"Uh … no. No, thanks. I was just thinking," his eyes flashed excitement and drew her in, "there's something unusual about the Hamilton place. Would you like to see the house?"

He'd connected with her, and she didn't want it to end. "Can we go tonight?"

"I've got a flashlight in my truck."

"Okay to bring Clover?"

"Of course."

"Since he's the first pet of the week, I left him in his kennel for the evening window shoppers."

They made their way downstairs.

"Hi, Clover. Ready for a walk?" Claudia picked up his leash.

Clover made a quick turnabout, furiously wagging his tail. When Claudia opened the kennel door, Clover ran out and jumped straight up into a startled Pete's arms.

"Trusting fellow," he said, cradling him.

"He's getting attached to you. And you know what they say about dogs being a good judge of character."

"Maybe he's daft."

"Stop that. You're talkin' about my dog."

Pete carried Clover outside. Claudia locked the back door with a click.

Had pot roast and a little brown and white dog managed to crack through Pete's iron shield?

"You know what would be neat?"

"Nope." Pete had a feeling he was in for a topic change. Claudia had halted in front of the dark Gardner Hamilton house and stretched out her arms.

Captivated by her animation, Pete waited for Claudia to continue. The fragrance of night-blooming jasmine that had overtaken the porch railing sweetened the night air. Her hair shimmered in the light of the full moon, hinting at unknown possibilities.

"You restore the houses, and new owners turn them into bed and breakfasts."

Pete glanced at the old homes huddled on the square. "Bed and breakfasts. That would go hand-in-hand with the Downtown Reconstruction Board's plans."

Claudia motioned to the Truman Hamilton house. "You could have a bed and breakfast too. That's an awfully big house for one person. Even if you have a family, there would be plenty of room for both."

"Hold up. I'll have enough to do just handling the restoration. Adding a wife, children, and strangers to spend the night—not to mention a pet that needs grooming—you're overwhelming me."

Claudia gave him a wide grin, "I understand. That's kind of the way I feel. Moving to a new town, setting up my apartment and the dog grooming business, and now there's the training class. Put it all together and it does feel overwhelming."

"Ready to see the house?"

"Ready." Her response reminded him of a soldier prepared to march into battle accompanied by his trusty dog.

"Watch your step." Pete put his hand on the small of Claudia's back to steady her. The front steps creaked objections to their weight. His hand, still touching her, sent confusing signals to his emotions.

"These stairs will be the first thing I tackle." Pete removed his hand quickly when Claudia stood safely on the porch. He unlocked and pushed the heavy door. It swung open with a mournful moan, yielding a musty, cave-like darkness.

"I'm glad you brought a flashlight. This place is spooky."

"Why are you whispering?"

"Uh …," she turned her volume up a notch, "just seems appropriate? You did say there was something unusual about the house."

Pete directed his flashlight down the long hallway, and up the staircase to the right to help Claudia get her bearings. "Follow me to the kitchen."

Claudia followed close behind. Clover clicked a brisk cadence with his toenails. Pete shined his flashlight over the blueprints still spread out on the kitchen table.

"I heard about this in an episode of *This Old House*," Pete said, "but never encountered it."

"The house has a ghost?" She was whispering again.

"No. No, no," he chuckled. "I guess I'm being too mysterious for your creative mind."

"What then? I'm dying here."

"There was a practice in many old homes of building a secret hiding place or secret room."

"Oh my gosh! This house has a secret room?"

"It does."

"Where is it?"

"Somewhere in the central part of the house."

"You don't know exactly?"

"Therein lies the special conditions of my contract. The access point is unknown. I must restore the house to its original condition *and* find the secret room. If I meet those criteria, the restoration agreement will become a sales agreement. Marigold and Petunia want entry to the room before they relinquish their rights."

"Have you looked for the room?"

"Not yet, but I will."

"How can you stand waiting? I've got you working on my little project when you could be unearthing a hidden room?"

Pete smiled at her enthusiasm. "I thought you would find the prospect of a secret room interesting. The Hamilton sisters were allowed to go in once but weren't allowed to see how to get in."

"Were they blindfolded?"

"Maybe. They remembered descending stairs." Pete pointed to underlined words on the blueprints. "Look at this notation."

Written in blue were the words "hidden room" with arrows pointing under the house.

"There must be a basement."

"No. I've looked under the house. The only things reaching the ground are brick supports and the chimney."

"So, it has to be inside the house?" Claudia flipped through the various elevation sketches. Pete could almost sense a heat beyond that of the warm summer evening emanating from Claudia as she studied the plans.

"Don't worry. I'm confident I'll be able to find the room once I tear out the partitions used to make rental apartments. Let me show you around."

The flashlight cast strange shadows but revealed a large deep porcelain sink with windows above, white painted cabinets, and a checkerboard linoleum floor. "During the day, this room is quite sunny and bright with tall windows nearly reaching the ceiling. The original gas stove still works, but the refrigerator, which was probably an ice box, is gone."

"You should be able to find a replica on the internet."

"Probably." He opened a door leading off the kitchen. "This door leads to a utility porch that still houses an old wringer washing machine." Pete shined the light on the washer's hand-cranked rollers.

"This could be a museum where you teach how things used to be done."

"I need to teach me first."

"We know that feeling, don't we, Clover?" Claudia picked up the little dog and rubbed his head.

Pete led the way back to the front entry and entered the room to the right.

"These front rooms were converted into one-bedroom rental apartments. This room was first used as a study and still has floor-to-ceiling shelving along one wall." He ran the light from floor to ceiling to show off dust-covered shelves. "Behind the study was the formal dining room, converted into a bathroom. All that plumbing will be coming out."

"That's a switch. People add bathrooms today instead of taking them away."

"True. But I need to follow the blueprints." He motioned for her to follow, and they crossed the entry hall to the opposite room. Their footsteps echoed in the empty rooms. "This room was the parlor and functioned like today's great room."

"Except their entertainment was sharing stories, playing parlor games, and listening to live music," Claudia said.

"You're right. Activities that would have promoted real family interaction. Not like the techno stuff we have today." Pete opened a door at the back of the room. "I've got another bathroom to tear out back here. Fortunately, there are two bathrooms upstairs in the original plan—a unique feature. One bath with indoor plumbing used to be a luxury."

"This place is going to be amazing when it's restored, but I'd try to convince the sisters to allow for at least a half-bath downstairs."

To have Claudia share his appreciation for the old home's potential warmed his heart.

"Want to attempt the upstairs in the dark?"

"You'll never hear the end of it if you don't show us the second floor." She hugged Clover. "We're enjoying this tour, aren't we buddy?"

The light from Pete's flashlight crossed Claudia's face and sent back a glint of light in her eye that hit him like a thunderbolt. She made him feel—he wasn't sure how to express it to himself—alive, maybe?

Pete led the way out of the parlor to the broad, carpeted staircase in the front hall. He ascended the steps slowly, holding the flashlight beam up high to broaden its coverage. The carpeting muffled squeaks and creaks on the stairs.

"The second floor has two bedrooms on the left divided by a shared bathroom. These were the smallest and cheapest rentals." They walked through them, then came to the room on the other side of the hall.

"The master bedroom." As they entered, a strange ambience enveloped Pete. Claudia stood next to him, and Clover hugged close.

"Wow, what a view!"

The night had grown cloudy, but the moon and one star escaped momentarily to wink at them. The room had a fireplace to the left with a bank of windows opposite. Together they gazed out the large windows overlooking the bayou. Streetlights cast golden circles on a little marina of rocking boats and reflected light on the harbor waters, doubling their brilliance.

"If you open a bed and breakfast, this room would make a perfect honeymoon suite." Claudia turned to face Pete.

The picture of a just-wed husband drinking in his bride's eyes lit by the moonlight left him speechless. *Say something.* "This room will be even nicer when I get these windows unstuck."

"Won't the windows open?"

The plight of dealing with old windows. Safe subject. "Old sash windows are wood and swell in humidity." Claudia was so close he could smell the sweet light scent of her hair. His skin was hypersensitive to her nearness, as if exposed to heat after getting sunburned. *Air. He could use air.* "Let me see if I can open one."

He set the flashlight on its side in the windowsill, angling the light on the window. He unlatched the lock and pushed. Nothing.

Claudia set Clover down. "Let me help."

She pushed up on one side, Pete the other. The window yielded an inch.

"Hey, progress."

Pete gave another hefty push and the window rattled upward several more inches.

"I'm going to have a time with these windows."

The breeze wafted in, toying with his senses and playing with Claudia's hair. The branches of a giant oak waved with the wind, and a cloud slid over the moon.

The shadow reached in the window, directing him to gaze at her face. The dim light deepened the green of her eyes into dark pools, inviting him to dive in. Pete swallowed hard to quench the unexpected yearning of his heart. The flashlight beam gave the room a warm, golden glow. Clover, seated at Claudia's feet, stood, twitched his ears, and gave Pete a blank stare.

Pete's arms seemed separate from his body. His hands grasped her shoulders.

Her lips curved to a smile.

Heat hit his hands making him drop them from her shoulders. In a moment, quick as he'd been knocked off the ladder, she launched his sensibilities into the outer atmosphere. Raising her chin, she closed her eyes. His hands tangled in her hair and he drew her close. He felt her breath. His lips grazed her cheek and then her lips—softly, sweetly, quietly. His emotions expressed in action instead of words.

The wind stirred.

Screeeech.

An oak branch scraped against the windowpane.

Clover jumped between them. His paw swept across the windowsill and sent the flashlight rolling toward the open window.

Claudia lunged toward the light and stepped on Clover's foot.

The dog yipped.

Pete grabbed for the light, Claudia bumped against the raised window, knocking its tenuous hold loose. The window slammed shut on Pete's hand.

The moon popped out from behind the dark cloud.

Clover howled. The dog's long sustained cry covered Pete's.

Chapter 12

"A kiss from Pete *and* a fancy dinner? Wow!"

Claudia jerked the phone from her ear to soften the sound of Elaine's excitement. Clover raised his head and then settled back near Claudia's feet at the kitchen table.

"I probably shouldn't kiss and tell, but I couldn't reach you yesterday, and I needed to talk to you before I explode. I'm not messing up the bagel making, am I?"

"You actually picked a good time. The egg bagels are baking, and I have a batch of cinnamon-raisin ready to go in the oven."

"Hallelujah. You're the only one up at five-thirty on a Saturday morning that I can talk to. Well, besides Clover." The dog's ears flicked, one eye opened, then closed. "He's up, sort of."

Claudia sipped her orange juice and eyed her comfort food. "I feel like the grilled cheese sandwich on my plate—warm, cozy, and squeezed."

"Give it up. I want details."

"We painted paw prints on some trim, I used a power saw, he came to my place for dinner, he showed me the Hamilton house that has a secret room, and he kissed me."

"Hold it. You sound like a gushing fire hydrant. Back up. Where does the big dinner at the restaurant come in?"

"That was last night. I'm filling you in on the night before."

"You're confusing me. I thought you had Kali over for dinner Thursday, and Pete took you on a special dinner last night? What am I missing here?"

"Other way around. Kali phoned from Birmingham and couldn't make it back in time, Thursday. I got together with her at a fancy restaurant, her treat, last night."

"You invited Pete to dinner at your place Thursday?"

"Right. Kali's idea."

Claudia continued, filling Elaine in on the home-cooked dinner, house exploration, and … the kiss.

"I think the kiss embarrassed him, but I thought it was nice. Really nice. He actually makes me feel … graceful. Until the window slammed shut on his hand."

"Is he okay?"

"His hand is black and blue and swollen, but he insists he's fine."

"Ahh. How can you top romance in a stately 1912 home, harbor lights, twinkling stars, a tender kiss … Wait a minute. Didn't you say something about a secret room?"

"The Hamilton sisters told Pete there's a hidden room in the house. He has to find it before they'll agree to sell him the house."

"They don't know where it is?"

"They know the room exists. They just don't know how to access it."

"Wow. Did you hunt for the room?"

"No, too dark. But I'd love to look for it with Pete. Especially, if he'd open up more. There's a softer side to him I'd like to get to know."

"He's hard to read but has a good heart. His ministry work is proof of that. Where did you and Kali go for dinner?"

"She went above and beyond to make up for missing my home-cooked dinner. We met with her hair stylist. Kali had her give me the works—facial, hairdo, manicure, and pedicure. I always thought getting a makeover would be neat, but at the same time I felt … I don't know … out of place."

"From what I've seen of Kali, that's part of her salesmanship—curb appeal."

"She needed to give me a makeover and call me a professional dog trainer to give me curb appeal?"

"I'm just saying that's probably the way she operates and wants to help you fit in."

"Her idea to help me fit into her world was a dinner cruise." Claudia closed her eyes and frowned at the thought. "I wilted just like a flower stuck in a sauna when I saw that ship rolling on the water. She must have seen the green under my make-up and took me to a bench to sit down."

"What did you tell her?"

"Only that going out on the water makes me queasy. I wasn't up to telling her my whole story."

Explaining her gripping anxiety over boats and traveling across large bodies of water wasn't her idea of a pleasant evening. What she did know is the water that lapped lazily at the base of that ship could become treacherous and destructive and suck the life out of those on board. The horror of her parents' fate had become her deepest fear.

"No need until you're ready," Elaine said. "A lot of people get seasick. I guess Kali was understanding?"

"She didn't seem to care about an explanation. We ate at a five-star restaurant next to the marina with amazing bread, seafood, and desserts." Claudia handed a bite of grilled cheese to Clover.

"Kali shared her hopes and plans with me. I can see why she'd like to impress Mr. Sterling."

"Mr. Sterling's the one who wants the dog class?"

"Yes. But I get the idea his *wanting* the class has come with some prodding from Kali. He owns Sterling Enterprises, which operates several businesses, including a large real estate firm. By helping get his dog trained, she hopes he'll take an interest in Southern Life Realty."

"Sounds like a promising plan."

"Promising is right. She promised my services, and Sterling is going to attend the class next week."

"Are you going to be ready?"

"I wanted the class at The Top to be a test class, so I would be ready for Sterling."

"Tell Kali."

"Just tell her it's not a good time?"

"Absolutely. You don't have to please everybody's whims. Learn to say no."

"You sound like Pete. I can't help it. Kali has been so nice to help me. She already told Sterling about the class. He's scheduled to be here for six weeks. This seems to be his window of opportunity."

"Then look on the bright side. If Mr. Sterling has time to work with his dog, all should go well."

But a dread managed to suck the air from her lungs. With Claudia's history, a looming concern told her the opposite was true.

Main Street had stirred to life, energized by the bistro traffic at 7:30 a.m.

Pete held the painted table he and Claudia had created and knocked on the front door of The Pampered Pooch.

"Ouch."

He set the table down, and rubbed his sore hand, still carrying the imprint of the windowsill. Hopefully, Claudia and he could remain friends and business associates. The kiss had seemed so natural. Yet what possessed him to cross his self-imposed boundaries? His father had warned him about getting too close.

The slamming of the front door had awakened him. Six-year-old Pete went downstairs and found his father sitting on the end of his bed—his back slumped, hands clenched. The closet, half empty, held only his father's clothes and shoes.

"Daddy?"

His dad straightened. "Son, what are you doing up?"

"The front door ... where's Ms. Linda?" That was the name of his latest live-in. There had been three, or was it four, since his mother left.

"Gone." His dad raised his big hand to tousle Pete's hair.

"Will she be back?"

"Son, you need to learn something that has taken me a long time to understand. If you get too close to a woman, you set yourself up for hurt."

He knew from his own experience he should take his father's advice. Why had he set himself up? There was something about Claudia that made him feel worthwhile—maybe even loveable. But his sore hand was a subtle reminder of his dad's warning. Romantic notions could be a relationship killer.

He knocked again.

Claudia peered around the corner of her apartment stairwell with Clover at her side. She held her cell phone to her ear. Her hair, piled loosely atop her head, tumbled down in coppery wisps that framed her face.

She tipped her head toward the front door and burst into a full smile. Phone propped on her shoulder, she hurried to unlock the door.

"Good morning," Claudia mouthed and pointed to the phone, "Francine."

"Oh, it's painted." Claudia's eyes lit up. "Francine, Pete's here with the project I was telling you about." She pointed to the magazines piled on the floor beside the sofa.

Pete set the table on the floor next to the stack. His plan had been to deliver the table and leave. So how come he was still here?

He'd seen her in a dress, with her hair pulled back, and make-up accentuating those green eyes, and thought she couldn't be more beautiful. But here she was—clean-faced, with her fetching freckles, in a casual T-shirt and jeans. She was lovely, period. And needed to be off his self-prescribed limits.

He turned to leave. Claudia grasped his arm and whispered, "Will you wait a minute?"

In the phone she said, "The food was terrific, pricey, but Kali insisted the dinner was her treat. They make an awesome cake full of nuts. Uh-huh. She's arranged for a businessman she hopes to impress to join our class next week. I'm glad you'll be there with Toby for moral support. Please pray all goes well."

Pete squatted down to pet Clover, who rested his head on Pete's knee. He ran his hand over his soft fur and studied the pattern on Clover's back. To make the design into a four-leaf clover took more imagination than he had.

"Yes, yes. Thanks." She ended the phone call and set the phone on the appointment table.

"Good morning. Sorry for the hold up." Claudia pulled at a tendril gracing her cheek and tucked it behind her ear.

"No problem, I just wanted to drop off your table."

"Imagine, we actually built this together from scratch." Claudia leaned down to inspect the table. "Impressive paint job too." She straightened. "I had a big night with Kali at Captain Anderson's restaurant."

From painted table to Kali in two seconds. He never knew where a conversation with Claudia might be heading. "Nice place."

"She had planned on a dinner cruise." Claudia inhaled, then released a quivery breath. "But I ... uh ... don't do boats."

"How come?"

Claudia balled her fists then released them. "It's ... that I can't ..."

He hated that she was so uncomfortable. He'd throw her a lifesaver. "So, you like the way our project turned out?"

"Oh, yes." Her facial expression brightened. She quickly sorted magazines and papers, arranged them on the end table, and stepped back. "What do you think?"

He couldn't say what he was really thinking. He'd like to be someone less even keeled and more exciting, but that would never be him. If she was the Kali-friend type, so be it.

"It gets your magazines off the floor."

"That's all you have to say, Pete Cullen? This table is unique—a great accent piece for the shop, and we built it together."

There was a light tapping on the shop door. Clover growled, bared his teeth, and lunged at the door, barking wildly. Claudia screamed. Pete turned to see a big black dog peering through the glass door. Then he caught sight of the tall, spiked heels.

"Kali?" Claudia pressed her hand to her chest and laughed. Clover continued barking. Pete lifted Clover from the floor. Claudia opened the door. The little dog's heart pounded with the intensity of a call-to-war drumbeat.

"How do you like him?" Standing beside Kali was a life-size ceramic Doberman pinscher. "He requires no walking or feeding."

"He's a beauty," Claudia said touching the fake dog's pointy ears.

"I found him at a special interiors shop on the beach and thought of you. And look what else I found." She reached in her pocket and presented a gold chain with a clover pendant.

"For me? How sweet."

"It's for luck."

"Really? Maybe a lucky charm is what I need."

"Pete, would you mind bringing in Claudia's new dog?" Kali asked as she hooked the necklace around Claudia's neck.

Pete set down Clover and eyed Kali with a what-are-you-up-to look.

Kali bounced an I-know-you-know-I-play-people-but-that's-how-it-is glance off Pete.

"Where would you like this dog?" Pete asked Claudia.

"Beside the appointment table."

Clover grumbled.

"Hush, Clover. He'll make a classy addition to the shop." Claudia adjusted the necklace to hang straight. "Thank you so much."

Kali gave a satisfied nod and looked around. "You've got this place looking colorful. That magazine table is a nice touch."

Claudia stood tall. "That's the piece that Pete and I built."

Kali flashed a smile, but her eyes didn't get the message. "Nice work. How's my doggie buddy?" She reached out to Clover.

Clover snapped at Kali's hand.

"Clover," Claudia scolded, "calm down."

"If I didn't know better, I'd say he didn't like me."

"He won't soon forget your bringing a devilish looking dog into his space," Pete said.

"He'll calm down when he sees the dog isn't real," Claudia said.

"Yes. Well, I ..." Kali brushed her hands together and checked her polished fingernails, "... came to see if I could put in some practice time with Clover and my dog trainer friend."

Clover growled again when Kali mentioned his name.

"Probably not a good idea this morning. We'll have to wait until he calms down. He's doing great with the sit, heel, and stay commands, though." She took Clover to his kennel. "Here you go boy. You relax for now."

Engrossed in conversation, Claudia and Kali seemed oblivious to Pete's presence. He cleared his throat and announced, "I brought the rest of the wood scraps. Want me to put them in your storeroom?"

"Sure, there's some space on the storage shelves next to the grooming supplies. Thank you. But hold up, I have your check ready."

Claudia bounded upstairs before he could stop her.

"I was going to tell her I could get it later," Pete said to Kali.

"I guess she's the type that likes to take care of her bills right away."

Kali looked away from the stairs and said, "Claudia tells me you've got a mystery to solve."

"How's that?"

Kali's phone rang. She pulled the phone from her purse. "Excuse me."

Pete went to his truck and got the extra scraps. He could have suggested building something else, but that would serve no purpose other than the danger of stringing along his feelings for Claudia. *Lord, help me rein in these emotions.*

He returned with the stack of wood scraps and small jars of paint. There was a rap at the back door. He parted the curtains, saw Emme from the florist shop with her little boy, and opened the door.

"Oh, hi, Pete. I didn't expect to see you here."

"Mama, can I see the doggie?" Richie asked.

"Okay. Pet gently." To Pete, Emme said, "I thought you'd be working at the Hamilton house with the publicity and all."

"Publicity?"

"In the *Talk of the Town* paper." She placed the folded newspaper on the appointment table. "I brought a copy for Claudia in case she didn't see the article."

What was she talking about?

"Activity around the park has picked up. Especially around the Hamilton house. People love a mystery."

Pete's body tensed. "May I?"

"Sure." Emme unfolded the paper and pointed to the headline. *The Hamilton House Holds a Mystery*, reported by Lyman Beardsley. Kali pushed in next to him. Her perfume heavy.

"Good old Lyman." Kali said. "You say the intrigue is bringing more people downtown?"

"I'd say so. I've had several new customers come into the flower shop," Emme said.

Pete stared at the article and became vaguely aware of Claudia's footsteps on the stairs. She greeted Emme. Pete frowned and gave Claudia a questioning look.

"You told people about the conditions of the agreement?" A heat flushed through his body.

Kali gave Claudia an awkward glance. A look she didn't wear well.

"Agreement? Oh, you must mean the secret room," Claudia giggled as if the confidence was between her and Kali instead of with him, as he'd intended. His stomach clenched.

"Finding the hidden room was supposed to be a secret?" Claudia asked Pete.

"The conditions of the Hamilton house restoration were strictly between the Hamilton sisters and me."

Pete spoke in an even, but firm, monotone.

"Richie, it's time to go," Emme said.

"Aww. Bye, Clover," Richie shuffled past him and exited the back door with his mother.

Kali smoothed her hair and straightened her jacket. "Listen, I've got some calls to make. Claudia, I'll touch base with you later."

Pete watched Kali retreat.

Claudia frowned. "You said yourself I'd find it interesting. I did. I only mentioned it to Elaine and Kali."

Pain struck Pete's jaw, and he realized his teeth were clenched.

"Finding the room was something special and private I shared with you." If she told Kali about the hidden room, no doubt she thought nothing of telling about his foolish kiss. He could be certain Kali and Claudia had a good laugh at his expense.

"Pete, honestly, I didn't think you'd mind."

"You're right. You didn't think." At least he wasn't foolish enough to tell her he had a map with an *X* that matched hers, or treasure hunters would be digging up the park. "Thanks to you, I've got curiosity seekers wandering around the house." Pete's steps fell heavy as he went to let himself out the front door.

"Pete, your check."

"Mail it," he said without looking back.

Inside his truck, he took a deep breath. What was wrong with him? He checked the reflection in his rearview mirror, half expecting to see a stranger. He needed to get a grip.

Pete had prayed his feelings for Claudia might be curbed. He wasn't expecting them to be severed.

Chapter 13

Claudia grabbed her dog obedience paperwork and some extra leashes and wished she could leave her misgivings in the car. Behind The Top of the Harbor, an outdoor picnic area had been cleared for the dog obedience class. Visions of Harvey romping after the cat and the bichons wrecking Elaine's grand opening steamrolled through Claudia's mind.

"Who am I to train dogs? I must be insane." Clover jumped up on his hind legs and rested his front paws on his cage. "You need to be good for Kali tonight."

With Mr. Sterling in attendance, she wanted her friend to appear competent. If Kali could set aside her cynophobia, surely Claudia could perform like the dog pro she used to be.

Her stomach was skittery and had been ever since Pete stormed out of her shop. He should have cautioned her if he didn't want her to say anything about the hidden room. How was she to know she was the only one he told? Kali had said not to worry. Pete could be unpredictably unreasonable.

"Pete was hurtful and unfair. Wasn't he, Clover?" Clover stilled his tail and cocked his head. He never once looked her way in church last night.

Claudia tried to swallow the lump in her throat. She couldn't think about his anger anymore. She had a class to teach. Kali had been her encourager, and she hoped the class would help Kali's status with Sterling.

Someone touched Claudia's shoulder. "Nervous?"

"Francine." Claudia bent and patted Toby's cute pug head. "I'm so glad you signed up for my class. I need a friendly face."

"You'll do fine. And Lake, my investigator friend you met, contacted someone who remembers your parents' boating accident and is willing to search for the case file and photo."

Claudia grasped Francine's soft hands and felt a burning sensation in her eyes. The tension of the evening and the possibility of receiving the photo of her parents pushed her near tears.

"Thank you so much." Claudia hugged Francine.

"Remember, we're a friendly group, and anything you teach us will be appreciated," Francine said. She fished a tissue from her purse and handed it to Claudia. "You're the one with the knowledge. Lord, bless Claudia and give her clarity of mind."

"You make praying seem so simple," Claudia said, wiping at her eyes.

"I believe God meant praying to be simple—like sharing thoughts and concerns with a friend."

Francine gave Claudia's hand a squeeze. "Come on, Toby, you better take a break before class starts."

Claudia smiled and thought about Francine's encouragement. Why be fearful? She had experience and a lot of knowledge about dog obedience. The way Clover was learning should be proof enough.

But there was her last class in Atlanta—the class that led her to swear off teaching dog obedience forever. Claudia closed her eyes. She could see the police arresting her. *No, no, no.* Why had she agreed to this class? Why couldn't she simply have told Kali no?

Lord, since I agreed to this class, please help me teach each person in a way that will truly help them manage their dog.

Other pet owners from the apartment building started to arrive with their dogs.

Dave Burbank made his way to Claudia with his reddish-brown Chihuahua. "Meet my little man, Charlie."

"Hi, boy."

Charlie stared at Claudia with deep brown eyes the size of marbles and trembled as if chilled in the eighty-degree summer evening air.

"Looks like you've got a nice turn out for your class. Charlie and I are raring to go."

"Good. We may need some of your enthusiasm, Charlie." The little dog yawned.

A black SUV wheeled into a parking space nearby. Kali stepped from the driver's side. Mr. Sterling got out of the passenger side carrying his canine protégé, Bitsy. The perky-eared, golden-brown Cairn terrier sported a red jeweled collar with sparkling brown stones that matched her hair.

Kali hurried over, flashing her winsome smile. Mr. Sterling attached a leash to Bitsy's collar. Bitsy led the way to a grassy area on the side of the parking lot, gagging as she pulled against Mr. Sterling's restraint. Claudia saw immediate pointers she could offer.

"You ready for your students?" Kali asked.

"I hope. The first thing Bitsy needs is a different collar."

Kali moved toward Clover's kennel while Claudia reached in her supply box for a small Martingale collar for Bitsy. Clover began a deep growl that rumbled louder with each of Kali's steps. She stooped to speak to him. "Ready to impress Mr. Sterling?" Clover barked sharp retorts.

"Clover, shush," Claudia said. "Remember our talk. You need to be good for Kali." Claudia patted Clover's front feet grasping the bars of the cage. "I think once he's out of his kennel, and we get started, he'll act better."

"I hope so." Kali turned to Clover, "See you soon, boy."

Clover complained.

"Good evening," Mr. Sterling said as he approached. His arm and leash were fully extended with Bitsy leading the way. He was a tall man with thick white hair and straight-backed posture. A man most likely accustomed to being in charge, except when dealing with his dog.

"Bitsy and I are reporting for school." He reeled the terrier in and scooped her into his arms.

"Mr. Sterling, I'm looking forward to working with you and Bitsy."

Mr. Sterling shifted Bitsy to his left arm. "Julius, please. And we look forward to working with you too."

Claudia held out the back of her hand for Bitsy to sniff. "So, this is the famous Yummy Bits doggie. I see your cute little face in the pet food aisle all the time, and I have something special for you."

Claudia held up the collar from her supply box. "This is a Martingale collar. I see that Bitsy is a puller, and Kali said she sometimes escapes. I think you'll find this collar is an excellent training tool."

"Sure, whatever you say, I'm willing to try." Sterling unhooked Bitsy's jeweled collar, and Claudia assisted in putting on the new one. "Martingales have a cinch loop that will restrict when Bitsy pulls on the leash, avoiding the possibility of escape." She patted Bitsy's furry head and made the proper adjustment for Bitsy's neck size, showing Sterling how to do it himself. "With this adjustment, the collar will tighten just to the size of Bitsy's neck without choking her."

Bitsy wagged her tail and tilted her head, striking the trademark Yummy Bits pose. Claudia hoped Bitsy's congenial response signaled a willingness to learn. Now, if she could just train the people.

Pete pressed the button next to Francine's apartment door and waited.

Ripping off sheetrock and pulling down partitions had helped work off some of the anger over Claudia's carelessness, but he didn't want to delay Francine's project any longer.

Pete buzzed the apartment again. He had left the Hamilton house early to install an under-cabinet light in Francine's kitchen. Where was she?

He noticed a note pinned to the grapevine wreath on her door.

Pete, if you get here early, you can find me outside in the patio area.

Walking down the hedge-lined sidewalk leading to the outdoor patio, Pete heard Claudia's voice, sending an electrical jolt to his stomach.

"… do your homework faithfully. Your dog learns by drill and consistent repetition."

From the vantage point of a break in the hedges, Pete could watch the obedience class without being noticed.

Claudia faced her students, Francine among them, and went over the basic rules of the class. Dressed in simple khaki slacks and a light-yellow shirt, Claudia looked sharp with Clover by her side. He was a perfect model when she demonstrated the proper use of the collar and lead. Kali stood to one side near a tall, barrel-chested man with white hair—Mr. Sterling, he guessed.

"Give commands with clear, peppy tones. Correct in low, gruff tones."

He'd been gruff with Claudia. But how could she have not known the secret room needed to stay a secret between them? He had to buy "No Trespassing" signs, post them around the property, and ask Jeff for extra police patrols.

Even so, he wished her well with the obedience class. From the cover of the Hamilton house, he had watched Claudia working with Clover the past couple of days. Not surprisingly, Kali had been nowhere to be seen.

He'd felt like a Peeping Tom but admired her natural patience and grace putting Clover through his paces. He had wanted to apologize. He'd rerun his harsh words to Claudia a hundred times, wishing for a different outcome. He was out of line. But there was no way to erase the argument. Besides, if he stayed away, he wouldn't have to keep his attraction to her in check.

"Start with your left foot for the dog to move with you, the right if the dog is to stay in place."

Claudia's coppery hair, pulled back with wispy ringlets cascading against her face, shimmered in the outside lighting.

"Go ahead and take your place." Claudia motioned for Kali to take Clover and pointed to the space next to her.

Kali obeyed, but Clover didn't.

"Come on, Clover. We need to mind Miss Claudia." Kali's voice quivered.

Clover glanced back at Claudia, sat down, looked at Kali and uttered a low growl. Kali shrugged her shoulders and turned her free hand upward as if pleading with Claudia.

Kali helpless? A hint of satisfaction hit Pete. *Where did that come from?* He knew how much this class meant to both Kali and Claudia.

Claudia gave Kali a reassuring look, and a hang-in-there wave of the hand.

"We'll start with the sit, stand, and stay commands."

As Claudia instructed, she went around the circle of students and observed.

Pete muffled a chuckle when he saw Dave with his tiny dog. "Charlie, hold up. You're sittin' before I tell you to."

Mr. Sterling's Bitsy stood and stared when he told her to sit. Claudia intervened and demonstrated. "Just put your right hand through her collar going from head toward the tail. Then slide your left hand down her back, over the rump, to the back of the knees while giving the command. Bitsy, sit."

Bitsy sat down.

"Good sit," Claudia said.

"Well, I'll be. Let me try that." He went through the same procedure as Claudia, and Bitsy dutifully sat down. "Incredible. I feel in charge."

While the others worked, Clover continued to balk. Kali put her hand on the back of Clover's neck, but the stubborn dog showed his teeth, snapped, and snarled.

"Whoa, doggie." Kali jumped and moved as far back as the lead would allow. Clover began yapping. A distracted Claudia stepped on a poor unsuspecting poodle's toe. The poodle and Claudia yelped, unleashing general bedlam and yowling around the entire circle.

"Sit." Claudia commanded using her gruff voice.

Every dog in the circle complied. Claudia wiped perspiration from her face and apologized.

Amazing as Claudia was to silence the dogs, Pete saw the class might be in trouble. He stepped from behind the hedges and asked, "Kali, need some help?"

"You could say that." Kali acted as if an attack dog had her pinned.

"Clover," Pete said. "Settle down, boy."

At the sound of Pete's voice, Clover stopped yapping and stood quietly but kept watchful eyes on Kali.

"Understandable you'd distrust a shady character like her." Pete teased, but the tone he used was soothing and calmed the jittery dog.

"Call me anything you want, as long as you quiet him down," Kali said in a hoarse whisper.

Pete took the lead, and Kali backed away.

"Okay, class, let's keep working," Claudia said with a nod of her head and eyes that glowed in Pete's direction.

"Just let him know I'm not the enemy." Kali said.

"Not a part of dog obedience training, I'm afraid." Pete put his right hand under Clover's collar and the dog promptly sat down. "How do you like that?"

"I think it's a conspiracy you two cooked up." Kali spoke in an agitated tone and stepped closer. Clover growled.

"She's really not so bad, Clover."

Claudia finished working with the others in the circle and joined Pete and Kali.

"Thank you, Pete. You're a lifesaver." To Kali, she said, "You may need to put in some extra time with Clover and me at the shop." Claudia moved on to check on the other students.

"I don't know." Kali's neck displayed a splotchy red.

Pete wanted to let out an unsettled growl of his own. "Claudia's right," Pete said. "Whatever you're trying to prove or whomever you want to impress," he nodded at Sterling still practicing the sit command with Bitsy, "*you* are going to have to put in the training time."

Kali pushed her cheeks into a pout.

What was he doing? Reprimanding Kali was futile. What she and Claudia did were none of his business. *Remember that.*

Chapter 14

"Pete might not want to see me, but I have to see him." Claudia glanced at Clover as she pulled on an old work shirt and jeans in her upstairs apartment. "After saving my class from disaster, the least I can do is go help him work on his restoration, right?"

Clover rotated his head to one side and stared—never one to interrupt.

"Besides, I want to get to know him better." Maybe she could catch him before he left the Hamilton house.

Claudia retrieved her shoes. "A few exchanged hand waves across the park during the past week doesn't cut it." Clover spun around doing his ritual dance at the sight of Claudia's outside shoes. He raced ahead of her with toenails clicking a happy, hopeful tune.

Claudia descended the stairs behind Clover.

With no more appointments, she hung the closed sign on the shop door. The pet of the week—a black poodle named Curly—was fed and kenneled. She refreshed Clover's water and put a scoop of Yummy Bits in his bowl. "You stay and be a good boy. I'll walk you and Curly when I get back."

Clover discharged a couple of soft snorts. She rubbed his head and went out the back door.

Claudia jogged across the park toward the Hamilton house. Pete's truck was parked in its usual place. Thanks to her, black signs with No Trespassing in red letters decorated the front porch and lawn. She heard hammering as she skipped up the repaired front steps and knocked on the front door.

"Pete. It's Claudia."

"Don't come in," Pete called out.

Claudia's apprehension evaporated. Relieved he would tease her, she pushed the door open. Metal clanged as it scraped against the door. Inside, a wavering ladder with Pete clinging to the top loomed like a great giant over her head. The ladder crashed against the staircase, and Pete flew through the air, landing in a pile of drywall rubble.

Claudia watched the spectacle in horror. "Pete! Are you hurt?" She rushed to him.

Pete gradually sat up, brushing sheetrock dust from his face and hands. "Didn't you hear me say not to come in?"

"I thought you were kidding."

Through a haze of dust, his blue eyes spoke exasperation.

Claudia sank down on the pile of debris next to Pete. "I can never get things right with you. You tell me things that I repeat and shouldn't, and then you tell me not to do something, and I do it." Claudia picked up a piece of the drywall which crumbled in her hand and fell back on the heap. "Either way I manage to mess things up. I'm so sorry."

"Forget it," Pete said and brushed at the chalky dust on his pants that added to the plume of dust hanging in the air around them. Claudia sneezed.

"But I can't forget. I came to apologize and help you. It's the least I can do after all you've done for me."

Pete grunted as he struggled to get up and regain his footing. He held his hand out to her. Claudia grabbed it and he pulled her up. His grip was strong and solid.

"What have I done?" It sounded like he wanted to add "to deserve this."

"You saved my obedience class from disaster."

"I'm glad things worked out."

"Besides, I've never apologized for talking about the secret room and—" Claudia stopped mid-sentence and stared in the direction of the staircase. "What in the world?"

Underneath the fallen ladder, a section of the staircase was sticking straight up. Claudia's heart sunk in her chest. "Oh, Pete. I broke the stairs."

Pete's boots crunched on the debris as he stepped closer to inspect. He balled his fists to his hips.

"No," he said softly, "you just found the entrance to the secret room."

Pete lifted the extension ladder, carefully leaned it against the wall of the entry hall and examined the stairs. "You must have hit a spring release."

"Oh, my."

The first twelve steps remained stationary. The next six steps looked like the open mouth of a great sea serpent. He peered into the gaping hole. "There's a staircase leading down. Can you hand me the flashlight by the front door?"

"Sure."

Claudia hurried to get the light, but Pete wouldn't rush this discovery. He'd make sure it was safe to explore.

Claudia handed him the flashlight, which revealed steps and a landing about eight feet below. He put his foot on the first step and pressed down. The stairs felt sturdy. He started to descend. "You stay here. Let me see how secure these steps are."

"Oh, Pete, be careful. This is exciting but scary."

At the bottom step, he breathed stale musty air. A sweep with the bright beam exposed a narrow, dusty passageway leading to a wall with an opening on the right.

"You are keeping me in suspense up here. What do you see?"

"Patience is a virtue," Pete called as he made his way down the narrow space. Around the corner he discovered a small room, about 10 x 12 feet, with a table, chairs, and shelving.

"Pete, talk to me. What's down there?"

Pete returned and shined the flashlight on the stairs.

"Come down and see for yourself."

Her running shoes, jeans, T-shirt, and face with round-eyed wonder gradually came into view as she climbed down the stairs.

"Awesome," she whispered as if she might disturb decades of quiet held captive.

Pete shined the light behind them. "This part under the stairs forms a passageway." He followed the light. Claudia stayed close. Her short quick breaths turned into a sneeze on the back of his neck.

"Sorry."

"Bless you."

"Thanks. It's kind of moldy down here."

Pete shined the light into the room at the end of the passage and made a quick inventory. Hardback books lined most of the walls from floor to ceiling. Shelves of glass jars filled with preserved food were neatly arranged next to a vintage blue-spotted enamel coffee pot, eating utensils, towels and linens, and other household goods. Four folded cots stood in one corner.

"The room could have been intended for use as a storm shelter."

Claudia leaned forward, her arms tucked tightly against her body. Then, taking a deep breath, she pointed to an inscription on the wall above the storage shelves. "Shine the light up there." She read in a whisper, "He that dwelleth in the secret place of the Most High, shall abide under the shadow of the Almighty, Psalm 91:1." Claudia exhaled. "Wow." Her voice barely audible.

Pete read the words to himself. His whole body filled with a warm sensation.

After a moment, he directed the light from the Scripture to the table. A candle in a holder rested next to a glass Mason jar full of matches. "The candle will give us more light. I wonder if matches lose their spark. Hold the flashlight."

Claudia stood close to him—her presence suddenly more significant than discovering the hidden room. Her citrusy floral scent brought life and energy into the stale, long undisturbed room. And not just the room. Pete moved a few inches away from her.

He unscrewed the lid of the glass jar and took out a box of matches. After three strikes, the match flamed, and Pete lit the candle giving the entire room a soft golden glow. The smell of sulfur from the match lingered in the still air.

"Look." Claudia shined the flashlight on the opposite end of the table.

Pete held the candle up. The light revealed an open Bible and journal, a fountain pen and small bottle of ink. Books were stacked on both sides of the journal.

Claudia stepped to the end of the table and read the title of the book on top of one of the stacks. "*The Gold Seizure of 1933*—interesting." From the stack on the right, she lifted one of the books. "Oh, Pete, this is a Bible engraved for Marigold Hamilton." She shined the flashlight on the book underneath. "And this Bible has Petunia's name."

"Twenty-first birthday presents. Marigold said that they were to be shown the entrance to the secret room when they turned twenty-one."

"A kind of rite of passage?"

"I suppose so." Pete set the candle on the table, lifted the Bibles, and set them aside exposing two papers—exact replicas of the map with the X on it. "Do these look familiar?"

"The map in my apartment. Margaret said the map was a copy of an original found at the flower shop."

Her words came out with a whispered intensity that matched his excitement. The wonder of the discovery seemed to bond them together.

"This map has to be significant," Pete said. "The copy in your apartment—the Hamilton sisters showed me the original that was discovered in The Flower Cottage."

"These copies with the Bibles appear to be set aside for the granddaughters."

Claudia shined the flashlight on the map. "There's writing on the bottom. Scripture. Second Samuel 17:19. I didn't notice Scripture on the copy I have."

"I don't remember seeing a Scripture on the original either."

"Maybe it was cut off the others or added to these. Let's look up the verse." Claudia said.

"Yes." Pete loved having her by his side to share in this discovery.

"That's Old Testament. Let's see ..." she turned the pages carefully, "I don't want to muss Marigold's Bible. Here it is. *And the woman took and spread a covering over the well's mouth and spread ground corn thereon; and the thing was not known.*"

Pete furrowed his brow. "The X may represent a well?"

"That was covered up," Claudia said in a hushed voice.

Pete caught a glimpse of Claudia's eyes, wide at the idea. "Whatever the maps represent, Truman Hamilton didn't count on dying before the girls turned twenty-one."

"Wouldn't the girls' father have known how to get in this secret place and about the map?"

"He was killed in World War II."

"What about their mother, Violet?"

"Petunia mentioned her, but Marigold shushed her up. Whatever the reason, the way to find this room and its contents died with the grandfather."

Claudia fell silent, then spoke in a thoughtful, almost brooding manner, "There is no guarantee of tomorrow."

Pete pushed the candle closer to the open journal. "You're right. I would think there would have been a will or an executor to handle important matters. Truman Hamilton was a businessman."

Claudia shook her head, "I know from experience that what *should* happen and what *does* happen are two different things." Her voice melancholy. "I can relate with my own parents."

"Your parents?"

Claudia reached for the journal as if touching the yellowed pages could make a connection to her own past. "They died unexpectedly in a boating accident."

Pete searched for the right words to say. "I'm … uh … sorry." He checked the urge to hug her close and shoved his hands into his pockets.

"I never had the benefit of knowing their final wishes—or thoughts. This journal and Bible remind me of my mom. She read a daily devotion and jotted down her thoughts every morning before she started breakfast. She had her Bible and journal with her when the boat …"

Claudia bit at her lower lip and sat in the chair where Truman Hamilton apparently did his Bible study. She set the flashlight on the table, illuminating dark corners in the room that hadn't been exposed in decades. Her posture spoke of a need for answers to unasked questions.

"I never saw them again. How incredible it will be for Marigold and Petunia to get these Bibles and see their grandfather's journal."

Pete took the chair beside her. "Losing both parents had to be unbearable."

Her voice sounded childlike, and her eyes glistened in the dim light. "I was nine. My Gramma took me in, then later Aunt Lucy when Gramma went in the nursing home. Aunt Lucy broke her hip, and I wound up in a children's home." She wiped at her eyes with the back of her hands. "After losing my parents at sea, I still get queasy at the thought of getting on a boat. Accidents and mishaps, the story of my life." She looked so vulnerable. Candlelight stirred shadows that played across her face.

"You really believe you're bad luck?"

She lifted her shoulders, "As far back as I can remember, bad things happen when I'm around."

Sharing in this room seemed natural, and Pete was ready to listen. He wanted to know more about this girl who hindered his thinking and made him stop and stare when he saw her. "What bad things?"

Claudia drew in a long breath before speaking. "Where do I start?" Her speech came out in a rush. "My dad lost an irreplaceable collection of fishing lures when I knocked his tackle box in the lake. Grandma's priceless antique vase fell off the mantle and broke when all I did was walk near it. On a camping trip, I picked up a leaky can of gas that left a trail and ended up catching the camp on fire, tents and all. Oh. And I got arrested for dog theft in Atlanta."

"You were arrested for dog theft?"

She sniffled. "Yes. I managed to gain the confidence of a dog theft ring who used ignorant me to sell stolen dogs. I gave the new dog owners free obedience classes when they bought a dog. So, I've earned my bad luck nicknames."

"My last words to my mother were complaints that I was a freak because of my big hands and feet." She held up her hands as proof. "Because of my accident-prone ways, my Gramma told my mother she ought to hang a bulb of garlic around my neck—some old Italian belief—to ward off misfortune."

Pete smiled. "I suspect that tradition got started by fathers to ward off boyfriends."

"Oh, I didn't need garlic to ward off boys. In high school, I was dubbed Cloudia. A guy I dated in college was on the verge of proposing when he lost his job, went in the military, and got shipped to the Afghanistan." The candlelight flickered. "You see why it seems a black cloud follows me around?"

"Sounds like self-fulfilling prophecy. Whenever negative things happen, your black cloud theory is confirmed."

She stiffened. "You think I bring adversity on myself? Elaine constantly tries to make me tone down negative comments."

"A good start." Pete studied her face etched with concern. "You ought to add a positive outlook too."

"Claudia snickered. "Just tack on a different label and things will change?"

"There's something you're not considering. The other day, I saw you walking and talking to a poodle."

"I didn't see you."

"I was working in the front room that overlooks the park."

"Ah. The dog would have been Curly, skittish when the humane society brought her in, but doing better now."

"See? You are especially programmed to work with dogs. What you see as negative could be a blessing. I've come to understand that God makes us as we are—not as someone else wants us to be—for a purpose."

"Misfortunes that trail me could have a purpose?"

"Could." Pete leaned forward. "You stepped on that dog's tail at your obedience class. But with one word from you to sit, every one of the dogs quieted and sat down. Not just anyone could have done that."

She gazed at Pete with a longing in her eyes. Pete knew the look—a yearning for purpose and understanding. "You know, I'd forgotten, but when I was at the children's home, I made the cheerleading squad because of my big feet. I could form a good base for pyramid stunts. And I was recruited as a trapeze holder for the Florida State University flying circus."

"There you go."

"I'm indebted to you for helping with the dog class." Claudia touched the four-leaf clover at her neck and crinkled her forehead. "Making a new friend with Kali has been another positive. Maybe the clover Kali gave me is what I needed too."

"You mean like your Gramma's garlic?"

"Oh, that was supposed to keep bad luck away. This," she touched the metal clover, "is supposed to bring good fortune."

"And one reason makes more sense than the other?"

"Oh, I don't know. I just appreciate Kali thinking of me. She even said if she moves to Birmingham I should join her and we could be roommates. I wish Gramma was still around to meet Kali. She would have liked her."

Great. Bad enough that Kali had Claudia hoodwinked, but he had managed to make Claudia see Kali as her hero. No need to try and warn her again. Kali had made her agenda to impress Sterling clear. Why should it be his concern? He'd keep his opinions to himself when it came to Kali.

Amazing enough was the fact he was relaxed talking to Claudia. As foreign as Claudia must feel viewing herself as positive, he wasn't used to being comfortable with conversation.

"What about you Pete?" Her tone sincere. "I've bared my soul, so it's your turn."

Pete shifted in his chair. He rubbed the back of his neck. His comfort level was short-lived. The walls of the underground room moved in, and the air grew warmer. "Getting back at me for putting you on the spot?"

Claudia smiled and nodded.

"I have a pretty uninteresting life. What would you like to know?"

"Hmm. What did you do on the oil rigs?"

His explanation seemed to interest her but led to "Wouldn't that kind of job be rough on a wife and family, since you're gone months at a time?"

"I suppose. But not an issue for me."

"So, have you ever been married?"

"No."

"Engaged?"

"No."

"Come on, give me something here. I'd really like to get to know you better. Serious girlfriends?"

She was fishing. Dropping hooks. Hoping to snag a bit of him that no one seemed to ever care to know. Reasons he had to remain comfortably in his existence as a bachelor. So far, Francine, who embodied grace and understanding, had been the only one he'd felt the liberty to share about his past relationships and hurts. But now Claudia sparked something deeper—a sense of freedom to connect heart-to-heart.

"I was infatuated with … a cheerleader … in high school. Does that count?"

"Sure. Good. Tell me about her."

"After she talked me into being her escort for homecoming court, my football friends—and the word 'friends' is questionable—told me she wanted me to ask her out. I finally drummed up the nerve one morning before school and blurted out my invitation in front of not only her friends but my football buddies." *Why in the world did he bring this up?*

"And …" Claudia coaxed.

He sat back in the shadows. "She laughed at me. Not a simple laugh, a ridiculing, cut-to-the-bone laugh."

"The kind you don't just hear. You feel. I would have been mortified."

Pete was mortified, all right … mortified he'd shared the humiliating event that still seared his emotions. The secret room, hidden in the depths of the old house, was drawing out confidences he had stuffed somewhere in the deep recesses of his brain. Their closeness had weakened his defenses. Claudia had that effect on him.

Pete nodded. "That event ended me asking girls out until …"

"Go ahead."

"There's little to tell."

"After all I told? No fair. Give me more. You quit asking girls out until …"

"Until I met Lidia, from Czechoslovakia."

"Sounds enchanting."

"Enchanting?"

"You know, castles and such."

"Castles aside, I thought we were headed toward a serious relationship until I learned the only reason she'd set her sights on me was as a means of legally staying in the States. She found a more exciting prospect, ditched unlovable me, and left. With two strikeouts, I decided not to go for a third."

Instead of sympathizing, as he expected, Claudia played turnabout.

"*Now* who's dwelling on the negatives?" Claudia pointed both index fingers at Pete. "Don't sell yourself short."

Pete lowered his gaze. "I can dish out advice, but can I take it?"

Claudia nodded, hesitated a moment, and reached out and touched Pete's hand, sending vibrations through his body. He raised his head. She spoke decisively. "You are courageous … confident … detail-oriented … committed … faithful … and a good listener."

"Clover could fit that description."

She gave him a nudge-punch to the arm. "Would you stop? Now, I have to add humble to your list. I'm telling you, there's plenty of girls out there who would love to date you."

His heart jumped. She believed what she was telling him. She saw good qualities in him. Her words were like a buttered biscuit to a starving man. He wanted to hold her, feel his lips touch hers again. *Idiot.* "Plenty of girls" didn't include her. What excited her was moving to Birmingham and rooming with Kali.

N-n-n-o-o, not interested. "I'm better off alone."

The chair scraped against the floor as Pete pushed away from the table and stood. The candlelight sputtered. "It's getting late. We'd better go. I have to notify Marigold and Petunia about the discovery of the room."

"Changing the subject?" Claudia asked with a hint of teasing.

"Yes."

Claudia stood and gave Pete's arm a soft squeeze. The effect of her touch penetrated his hidden hurts. "I want you to know that the discovery of this secret place will remain a secret as far as I'm concerned. I'm sorry I spoke out of turn earlier about the hidden room."

"My fault. I assumed you knew the existence of this room should be kept confidential. I shouldn't have gotten angry." He flicked on the flashlight, and blew out the candle. Would the evaporating puff of smoke carry this interlude into nonexistence? He directed the light in front of them as they made their way back through the stuffy corridor. When Claudia put her foot on the first step of the ladder, she froze.

"Pete." She sounded startled.

"What is it?"

"Knocking you off the ladder?" She put it to him as a question, as if she needed to jog his memory. "My bungling actually helped you find the secret room. Another positive."

"You could say that."

They emerged from the opening in the stairs, and he glanced at the pile of sheetrock he'd fallen into. The fall left him addled. Beyond the rubble, he could envision Claudia as his wife, chatting at the Hamilton house kitchen table with Clover sleeping underneath. He could pretend he should avoid her for his physical safety, but the real dangers of being around Claudia were the pictures she drew on his mind and the emotional trauma she inflicted on his heart.

Something had changed inside him in the depths of the secret room, and he desperately wanted to tell her. But now was not the time. He had the downhearted feeling that there would never be the right time. She would return to her shop and Kali's influence. He would go back to his restoration work. Whatever he felt or imagined had happened between them would remain entombed in the darkness.

He swallowed hard. In the light, he'd regain his satisfaction with bachelorhood.

Chapter 15

Claudia inhaled a whiff of the strong coffee before she took a sip—bitter like her disposition. The morning sun's slanted rays coming through her apartment windows chose to pick on Clover lying in front of the kitchen sink, so he sought shade under the kitchen table. He slid his front and back paws outward until his tummy collapsed on the cool wooden floor.

Clover had to share Claudia's attention with Corky, the latest adoptee-to-be. After their morning walk, Clover's energy seemed zapped. He looked like she felt—downtrodden and forlorn.

Adding some water to her cup, Claudia reheated her coffee in the microwave and tried to refocus on her devotion. Finding Truman Hamilton's Bible and journal had sparked the memory of her mother journaling. Claudia had been jotting down her own thoughts in a spiral notebook ever since the discovery of the secret room. Five weeks ago. She could count on one hand the times she'd seen Pete. And not use all the fingers.

Was he avoiding her on purpose or just busy? Maybe after hearing all her hang-ups he decided she ranked two steps below poison ivy. She couldn't blame him. She had knocked him off a ladder—twice. But still, they had drawn closer—made an important connection—hadn't they? Did he think she was too dangerous to be around?

She straightened the clasp and pendent on her clover necklace. At least Kali had stuck by her.

"Clover," Claudia held up the charm, "you think this clover helped me have a successful five weeks of dog obedience school?" Clover raised his head, stared, and then rested his chin on his front paws.

"I'm sorry I had to leave you here, but it was you or Kali. If it weren't for Kali, there would have been no success with Bitsy, and Mr. Sterling would never have been inclined to donate a van to the church."

Clover rolled to his side and sighed.

"I hope you understand."

She pressed the button to pop the microwave door open, retrieved her warmed coffee, and settled down to ponder the morning scripture. Her daily routine now was to walk Clover and the doggie in the window at first light, jog on the treadmill, eat breakfast, have quiet time, and walk any boarded pets.

Today's boarders were the infamous duo, Corky and Fritz. She needed body and soul fortification before venturing out in the heat and humidity with those two. Each day she tried to glean what God had for her as she reread the Scripture. She was always grateful to get sound advice, and today was no exception.

The psalmist in chapter 119 had her feelings pegged. Her soul was breaking. The Bible writer longed for God's laws. She was aware of a profound need inside of her but unable to identify it. The yearning for something waiting to be discovered lay on the fringes of her mind, refusing to come out of the shadows. Was there some law or command she wasn't following? She couldn't pinpoint the emptiness that had created a black hole deep in her spirit—thirsting but never satisfied.

She pushed away from the table, her coffee gone cool again. The chair scraped against the wood floor, reminding her she needed to get some felt tips to prevent scratching. Between dog grooming, pet adoptions, the obedience classes coupled with church and activities with Kali, she had little time left for her to-do list.

The phone rang. Kali.

"Let's make it 5:30 at the beauty shop instead of 5:00. I have a late showing."

"Why not skip the beauty shop?"

"Not an option. It's essential. Like brushing your teeth. What if your clients quit grooming their pets?"

"I just clean and maintain their natural good looks. I don't make them into something they're not."

"But for us, that's the whole deal. Without makeup and a weekly hair touch-up, my mirror tells me to go away."

"It's a good thing my mirror doesn't talk to me. But 5:30 it is."

Claudia tugged a stubborn curl behind her ear. Zapping her wavy hair with a straightening iron lasted only until she stepped outside the beauty shop into the humidity. She examined her nails, the polish worn and chipped from scrubbing and combing out dogs. She wasn't cut out for the country club scene, but Kali was intent on trying. At least Kali and Mr. Sterling started coming with her to church supper and Bible study on Wednesdays.

The microwave beeped. She removed the cup. The aroma of the coffee in the rising steam and the feel of the cup in her hand was reminiscent of the special dinner with Pete. His napkin sketch of Feldman square still lay on the counter, reminding her of the touch of his lips on hers the night he told her about the secret room.

Finding the room was wild and amazing, but the weeks since had been a letdown. She'd told no one about their find, not even Elaine.

Claudia returned to the table and set down her coffee. What was the source of her unrest? Not seeing Pete? Not understanding why he didn't stop by to see her? Both?

"We miss Pete, don't we, Clover?" The mention of Pete's name set the little dog's tail in motion. Claudia moved her hand to stroke Clover, clipped the handle of her cup and spilled hot coffee on her shoe and Clover's tail.

"Yikes."

Clover jumped and let out a soulful yelp.

"Oh, sorry, buddy." She ran to the fridge for ice and tried to cool Clover's tail. "The ice will numb the hurt, boy. I promise." She dabbed at the spill on her shoes with a damp towel. "It's not safe around me. Pete is wise to keep his distance. I might as well forget coffee this morning—too hot outside, anyhow." She finished cleaning the spill and set the cup in the sink. "Let's go downstairs. It's the bichon brothers' turn for a walk."

Clover led the way down the stairs that Pete had admired. The cubicles over the kennels were more reminders of Pete.

Claudia sniffed the air. "Shew ... burning those dog biscuits again yesterday left a funny smell down here. I might as well stop pining away about Pete and see if I can freshen the air."

Claudia shuffled through items on her supply shelf and located a scented candle. "Peaches and cream." She grabbed matches, lit the candle and placed it on the shelving behind her appointment table. "That should help things smell better."

Clover wagged. The bichon boys wiggled furry tails. "Good. I'm glad you guys agree."

She hooked Corky and Fritz to their double leash and reminded herself to talk to Olivia about trying them on separate leashes.

"Let's go, boys. We might get lucky and run into Pete."

Smack.

Pete dropped a couple of two-by-fours onto a stack of lumber. The sound echoed across the backyard of the Hamilton house. He planned to repair the railing on the steps leading from the rear utility porch.

He checked the time. Claudia walked dogs at 6:30 and 7:30. When he worked on repairing the window sash cords in the front rooms, he could set his watch by her. Now, her walking habit had become his chance to get to see her, though he knew it was dumb to torture himself.

Ever since the night they shared secrets, Pete had known he was falling in love with the quirky girl that sported wild flaming curls. Why else would he think of her night and day and replay the kiss between them?

Yet, Kali was working to create a different girl. Elaine had filled him in on Kali and Claudia's weekly schedule.

"Tuesdays, Claudia meets with Kali at the beauty shop that specializes in makeovers before they go to dinner at the country club with Mr. Sterling. Claudia looks amazing. Kali convinced her to straighten her hair and add blonde highlights. Combined with makeup to cover her freckles, she could pass for Kali's sister."

"Claudia looks fine the way she is."

"Well, she did draw the line at fake nails. She said they'd be like weapons when she scrubbed dogs. But Claudia is enjoying her new friendship. Kali told her she was her good luck charm, because Mr. Sterling is so appreciative of the success Claudia's had training his dog."

"Kali needs a good luck charm?"

Elaine shrugged. "I guess. Claudia was convinced she brought people nothing but bad luck, so hearing she brought someone good luck has given her a new outlook."

"Humph. More like look out," Pete muttered.

"Why? Claudia's not the only one getting a makeover. Did you know she got Kali and Mr. Sterling coming to church supper and Bible study on Wednesdays?"

Pete didn't want to confess he had seen them. He was so troubled by Kali reshaping Claudia, he couldn't bear to watch. He shook his head. "I volunteered to deliver meals to the homebound."

"That's important too. I don't know how the Helping Hands Ministry would manage without you."

"Just fine. Anybody could do what I do."

Elaine laughed. "What am I to do with you *and* Claudia? She thinks she's bad luck, and you think you're inconsequential. The truth is, I see your contributions in this community as a God thing."

A God thing? Elaine's words stuck in his mind. Was God in the changes he saw materializing in Claudia? He'd seen her with smooth hair and a fitted dress—a replica of Kali—when Sterling picked them up on country club nights. Perhaps God was nudging her to another level. Maybe Kali's influence would help Claudia to no longer view herself as a freak, which was so far from true.

He couldn't know Kali's true motivations or God's purpose. After all, if Kali hadn't hooked Sterling up with Claudia, it's highly unlikely he'd have donated a van to the church. And also unlikely Pete would be outfitting the van for mobile dog grooming at Kali's request to surprise Claudia. No way he could compete with Kali's influence. It was best he remained detached.

Yet, he ached to see Claudia. She had invaded his heart and threatened to crumble his protective wall, like the walls he'd beat down in the Hamilton house, leaving piles of dusty rubble. He was reduced to catching glimpses of her in the early morning—hair a mass of curls pulled away from her face with no makeup. She was herself. The way she was meant to be, as far as he was concerned.

He walked around the side of the house with a view to the bayou in time to see the notorious Corky and Fritz twosome lunge after a squirrel.

"Whoa, boys." Claudia hung onto the leash while the dogs hurtled into a vine-covered thicket beside the old Feldman house. Claudia disappeared into the hedges.

Woof, woof. Yip, Yip.

"Ow, ow, ooow!"

Pete ran. "Claudia?"

He reached the bushes tagged with a torn piece of Claudia's shirt.

"Claudia are you okay?"

"My foot's stuck."

Pete plunged into the bushes, ignoring the thorny vines scratching his arms. The dogs, the leash, and Claudia were in a tangled wad. The disturbed layered mat of decayed leaves smelled musty. "Don't move. Let me look."

"I don't think I *can* move."

The dogs panted with quick, jerky saliva-dripping breaths. An annoyed blue jay screeched from an overhanging oak branch. Pete pushed back unruly branches until he could see where Claudia's foot was caught. His hand hit something hard. The rear legs of the dogs were underground.

"There's some kind of hole here."

Pete reached toward Claudia's ankle covered by Corky's fluffy rump. "Your foot is caught in a metal ring. Can you slide it straight back?"

Claudia strained to move. "My shoe is wedged tight."

"You stay still. Let me get the dogs out and tie them up. Then, I can see how to help you better. Come on, boys. You've had your fun for the day. Out with you."

Pete maneuvered the dogs out of the mass of vine-covered, broken branches, secured them around a nearby tree, and returned to Claudia.

She had scraped a clearing with her other foot. "My foot is stuck in a ring on a metal cover."

Pete touched her ankle. "Are you in pain?"

He felt her light touch on his back. "No. My shoe is just crammed in too tight."

"Let's go at it from a different angle. Let me help you stand up."

Pete got behind Claudia. The lavender scent of her hair intoxicated him as he reached his arms under hers and helped her stand.

"Maybe we can get your foot out, and free your shoe."

Pete untied her shoe as far as he could. "Okay, wiggle your foot free."

Claudia pushed against Pete's shoulders, while he pulled.

"It's moo ... ving." Her foot popped out. "There. Pete. You're a lifesaver." She flung her arms around his neck. The press of her against him drove his heart rate up quicker than a fifty-yard sprint.

He held her, experiencing the role of protector and liking it way too much. When he stepped away, he put his hands on her shoulders. "I'll get your shoe."

"Thanks. What do you suppose this is? An underground tunnel?"

"Most likely an old well that's been capped off."

"Youch. This sock doesn't give much protection from these thorns."

Pete freed the shoe with a couple of whacks. He knelt at her feet. "Hang onto me and step in."

"I feel like Cinderella."

"Cinderella got her foot stuck in a well cover?"

"No, silly. The part where the prince is trying to find the girl whose shoe is left behind at the ball. Only with my big foot, I'd be cast in the role of one of the ugly stepsisters."

"Hold up, Cinderella. Did I hear negative speak? You're just right the way you are."

"And you'd make a perfect Prince Charming."

"Ah, the beauty of it all amidst the thorns and thistles. And a tennis shoe replaces the glass slipper."

"I've missed seeing you," Claudia said.

"Have you now?"

"Are you avoiding me?"

The answer was yes but not that he didn't want to see her. "We've both been pretty busy. Elaine's filled me in on your schedule."

"I have been crazy busy. Last night was my last obedience class, and guess what."

"Uh … I'm not a good guesser."

"Mr. Sterling was so pleased with the results on Bitsy, he's donating a … are you ready?"

Pete nodded. Her excitement was cute as a pup with a new toy.

"A van. He's giving it to the Helping Hands Ministry at the church and wants me to use it for mobile grooming."

"Really?" He didn't want to spoil her surprise by telling her he'd been knocking off work on the Hamilton house early to refit the van for dog grooming.

"Kali told him I was interested in providing service to the elderly."

"Nice of her." The gesture was a nice one. But he still couldn't help wondering if Kali had an ulterior motive.

"Nice? Not just nice but splendiferous, if there is such a word." She gave Pete's arm a gentle punch. "Come on. Give me some enthusiasm." Claudia put her hands on her hips. "You're due credit for the van too, you know."

"Why?"

"If you hadn't saved that first dog obedience class, none of this would be possible. I ended up leaving Clover at home, and guess who became the star of the class?"

"I'm not a good—"

"—guesser. I forgot. So, I get to tell you. I used Bitsy for demonstration. She trots alongside Mr. Sterling now instead of pulling him. He is button-busting proud of his dog."

"And I'm sure Olivia would get the same results if she enrolled Corky and Fritz in your class. I'm proud of you."

"You are?" She smiled. Then, wide-eyed, her expression changed. Kali hadn't modified Claudia's amazing capacity to switch emotions in the space of a breath.

"Pete, the map."

"The map?"

"The framed drawing in my apartment, could this hole be the X?"

Pete pictured the drawing and furrowed his brow. "If the rectangle on the drawing represents the park, you might be right. One thing is for sure, it's a hazard. I'll get this roped off so no one else is injured."

"Wouldn't that be something if we solved the mystery of the X?"

The wail of a siren sounded. A black and white police cruiser turned off Main Street, sped around the park, and squealed to a stop beside them. Jeff reached across the front seat and thrust the passenger door of the police car open.

"Get in, Claudia. Your shop is on fire."

Chapter 16

Hot, humid wind gusts curled through Claudia's hair, giving fair warning the weatherman's promised morning thunderstorm was at hand. At least it was fresh air compared to the lingering, stale smell of smoke in her shop. She covered the two blocks to the bistro in record time, curious to find out why Elaine sounded so anxious to see her.

"I was about to get on the treadmill when you called, so I jogged down here instead."

Claudia patted her face with the towel she'd draped around her neck.

"Here's a mocha frappe on ice to cool you down."

"Thanks." Claudia slid onto a stool at the counter. "You said you needed to show me something?"

Elaine nodded, her expression grim. "I do."

She reached under the counter and pulled out a folded newspaper. "First, let me emphasize that the readership for this newspaper is not high. She slid the *Talk of the Town* paper in front of Claudia and flipped it open to reveal bright red letters on the top of the front page, *Fire Smokes Out Accused Dog Thief.*

The headline rushed over every nerve in Claudia's body, like a spark igniting lighter fluid. The memory she never wanted to revisit lay raw and exposed.

"But who? Why?"

"Lyman Beardsley. He has *Enquirer* aspirations and likes to practice outlandish headlines in this little weekly paper."

Claudia grasped the frosted glass. The sudden coldness struck at her core.

The officers had walked in the Atlanta dog shop, unexpected. The two men, dressed in dark slacks, white shirts and ties, flashed official looking badges and plunked a search warrant on the counter. Their mirrored sunglasses reflected Claudia's gaping mouth.

"You sell and issue the papers on these dogs?"

"Yes."

Bad answer.

One officer rattled off, "You have the right to remain silent, anything you say can and will be used against you …" The other pulled her arms behind her back and clasped her wrists in handcuffs. She was led out of the shop, paraded before the stares of onlookers.

"Did you know you can't blow your nose when you're in handcuffs?" Claudia sniffed and wiped her runny nose on her shirt printed with *The More People I Meet, the More I Like My Dog.*

Elaine grabbed a napkin and handed it to her. "News to me. Important thing is, the owners of the shop were at fault, and you were released. Jeff saw the paper on the newsstand early this morning."

Claudia frowned. "But the only ones who knew about the dog theft ring are you and Jeff … and Pete. Would Pete—?"

"I can't believe Pete would tell Lyman." Elaine said.

Claudia read the opening paragraph.

Claudia Stewart, new owner of The Pampered Pooch, was hampered last week with a fire that smoked up her shop. But when the air cleared, Talk of the Town discovered an arrest in the dog groomer's background. Ms. Stewart ran a dog shop in Atlanta and was arrested for involvement in a dog theft ring. Expensive dogs were stolen and sold with counterfeit pedigree documents for big prices from her store.

Now, Talk of the Town begs an answer. Will her past affect her future and our chances to grow Main Street?

Claudia slapped the paper against the counter. "Just when I thought I was making inroads here. Dealing with the burned curtain from the scented candle and a soot-covered shop has been devastating, but this—"

"Listen, most people know this is a rogue paper and pay it little attention. Jeff and I just wanted you to be aware, in case someone asks about … you know … the dog theft."

"I know I shouldn't say it, but my infernal black cloud—"

"Will blow out to sea. You'll see."

Rrring.

"Can you get that, Aunt Lucy? I'm on a ladder."

"Will do."

"Pampered Pooch. Yes. Okay, would you like to reschedule? All right." Aunt Lucy hung up. "Another cancellation."

Claudia climbed down the ladder and washed out the rag she was using to clean the ceiling fan. "That makes the third cancellation this morning. Elaine said that paper had limited readership. If the readership is limited to people with dogs, I'm in trouble."

O'Flannery, already cleaned of soot, gave her his ever-present wink.

Sponge in hand, Aunt Lucy returned to her work removing the black stain clinging to the walls in the back-entry hall. A large floor fan hummed in the open back door, clearing out the remaining acrid smoke odor from the week-old fire.

"Thanks to your help, I believe the soot is about gone," Claudia said. She poured dirty water from a bucket and watched the liquid swirl about and disappear down the drain. "I hope that doesn't mean my business has gone down the drain too."

"You have too many people pulling for you. This ordeal will pass, you'll see."

As Claudia refilled the pail, her elbow clipped a container of grooming combs, scattering them on the floor. Clover scrambled to get out of the way.

Water sloshed on the hardwood floor as she plunked down the bucket to pick up the combs. "Is this to be my life? One string of mishaps after another?"

Unruffled, Aunt Lucy said, "You mop up the water. I'll get the combs."

Claudia struggled for a positive thought. "At least this part of the floor will be clean."

Aunt Lucy matched her attitude. "If this fire had to happen, at least it was before I left for the Octoberfest Volksmarch next month in Georgia, or I might not have been able to help."

"Yes, and *if* I hadn't burned the dog biscuits, I wouldn't have left a candle burning. Ifs are depressing." Claudia grumbled and mopped.

Claudia rinsed out the rag she used to wipe the floor and pulled another rag from a stack to dry the floor. Cleanup had been completed in increments, so she could keep her shop open. Now, it was looking as if staying open might not matter.

Her appointment calendar was filling with cancellations. "Sorry, but I need to cancel Peppy's appointment. I'll reschedule later." " Plans have changed, no need to board Princess this weekend." "I can't make it for grooming today. Sorry."

Everyone was sorry but not as much as she was to have her dog theft arrest exposed. She wanted to crawl under a rock and never face the public again. "Why do people feed on the misfortune of others?"

"Don't waste your time worrying about that sleazy paper. The past doesn't define you. The townspeople will come around when they learn the truth," Aunt Lucy said.

"I doubt the truth will make it into print. Even if there's a retraction, the article wouldn't come out for a week and would probably be buried in the classifieds. Who will notice? Bad luck tracks me like a hound dog on a trail."

"Look at the blessings."

"What blessings?"

"Are you forgetting all those who pitched in to help since the fire?"

She was right. When word spread that the damage would be less than the $2,000 deductible on her insurance, ladies from Francine's Sunday school class and men from the Helping Hands Ministry pitched in and scrubbed the main shop from ceiling to floor. Dave brought the large floor fan. Emme and Izzie cleaned and placed fresh flowers in the display window. Elaine sent food for all the helpers. Even their policeman friend from college, Tony, sent an IOU for any help, since he was out of town taking a law enforcement class.

"I am blessed. The fire could have been worse, and I've been fortunate to have the help of so many, especially you."

"Shows you who your real friends are."

Claudia nodded. "Pete has been wonderful. He removed all the kennel covers, cleaned, and returned them before you arrived. He even pitched in to help Dave's crew with cleaning the ceiling, but I insisted he leave. He has his own restoration project."

"What about your real estate friend who talked you into giving the dog obedience class? I haven't seen her around."

Claudia squeezed black, greasy mess from a sponge. "She sent someone from her rental cleaning crew to steam clean the sofa. Kali's work has been keeping her busy."

"After spending all that time with you, now she's suddenly busy?"

"And your point is?"

Aunt Lucy pressed her lips into a line. "The air in here definitely smells cleaner. When you look at the blessings, it helps you see that good can come from bad."

"I never thought I'd see this fire as good but—"

The shop door opened, and Kali breezed in.

"Your sofa is ready. My cleaning crew will deliver it today." She stopped and did a doubletake, seeing the freshly cleaned walls and shelving in the rear of the store. "Say, you two do good work. I could get you a job with Kristal's Kleaning Krew, if you're interested."

Aunt Lucy acknowledged the quasi-compliment with a cool "where-were-you-during-the-hard-work" nod.

"We are honored, I think?" Claudia said.

Kali shifted gears quickly. "Tomorrow night is the annual reunion for athletes from my high school graduating class."

"You were an athlete?"

"A cheerleader. Pete played football, and Lyman ran track. They'll be there too."

"Speaking of Lyman and running, I could do without him running his mouth. Did you see this?" Claudia held up the *Talk of the Town* newspaper.

"That's Lyman. He keeps his ear to the ground. Anything you say is subject to making it into one of his headlines."

"But the only person I shared that dreadful arrest with of late has been Pete. And he would never—"

"I've learned to never say never. Could be retribution for your slip about the secret room." Kali shrugged. "Anyway, forget Lyman. Nobody pays attention to half of what that paper prints."

"Forgetting what Lyman wrote is kind of hard at the rate of cancellations I'm getting."

"Well, if that article does hurt your business, I may have the solution. Mr. Sterling wants us to work with him in Birmingham."

"Us?"

"I think he considers us a team. He wants to add Southern Realty as an affiliate to his real estate business."

"Wow. Just what you've hoped for. But what could I offer? I don't know anything about real estate."

"Oh, you wouldn't work in real estate. Mr. Sterling wants you to work for his Yummy Bits company, in marketing."

"Sterling might not be so eager to hire me if he sees Lyman's story."

"Mr. Sterling is the one who told me he checked the arrest story and knows you were wrongly accused."

"He did? But ... the story just came out yesterday."

"Yeah ... well ... uh ... I guess news spreads fast. Anyway, all the more reason to get out of this negative publicity and start fresh in Birmingham."

"You think so?" A fresh start is what she'd hoped for in Hamilton Harbor. She had made inroads in the community, but news of her dog theft charge was apparently surging along those same roads, steamrolling her reputation. "But the van donation to the church for the mobile grooming—I can't let the church down."

"Listen, the Helping Hands Ministry can still use the van. Mr. Sterling can provide another mobile grooming van for you and ready-made clients in Birmingham when you agree to come."

"He'd provide another van?"

"Sure. He owns a Dodge dealership in Birmingham. The donation is some kind of tax write-off for him. Hammering out an agreement is why I have been so busy of late." Kali raised her chin and glanced at Aunt Lucy. "I just had to let you know so you could be thinking about the proposition. We need to stick together. You're still my good luck."

"Humph. I don't believe in luck, only hard work and perseverance," Aunt Lucy said as she rinsed out her cleaning sponge and washed her hands. "If you'll excuse me, I'm going to take a shower."

"Of course." Kali said.

Aunt Lucy stepped over Clover and said, "Claudia, did you know this dog has the outline of a heart on his rump?"

"Oh. No," Kali said, "if you look at him from the front, the brown splotch looks very clover-like." Kali stepped forward to point at the clover shape but jumped back when Clover growled.

Aunt Lucy raised her shoulders, glanced at Claudia, and shook her head. "I don't see it," she said, and continued up the stairs.

"I've got to go, but think on the Birmingham offer, will you?" Kali hurried out and closed the door behind her. The "open" sign plunked against the door glass.

Claudia patted Clover. "No matter, heart or clover, I love you just like you are." Clover thumped his tail against the floor and kept an eye on the door Kali just exited.

Like Aunt Lucy, Pete had seen a heart on Clover. And she'd felt her heart had been knit with Pete's in a special way that night in the secret room. Is it possible she'd read him wrong? Did he hold an underlying grudge about her telling he had a secret room to find? Was his helping clean the shop after the fire just an obligation to the Helping Hands Ministry? It could explain his standoffish attitude. Maybe small-town living wasn't for her. Gossip and rumor could land a serious blow in a heartbeat.

The shop phone rang.

Another cancellation? Maybe moving to a big city, where sheer numbers made a dog theft arrest of little consequence, was something to consider.

"Hello?"

"Claudia, this is Francine. Lake Spencer accessed your parents' case file. I have an envelope for you."

Pete, with fellow classmate and oil rigger, Kevin Underwood, arrived at the Sand Dollar Inn for the reunion on the hotel's boat shuttle. The sun hung low and large, creating a glare on the rippling water.

"How's the house restoration coming along?" Kevin asked as they went to their assigned drink station.

"Slow," Pete said.

In truth, the restoration had slowed to a crawl. Marigold and Petunia were ecstatic over locating the secret room and wanted time to process the find. "I'm working on the outside of the house, and I'm also custom outfitting the interior of a church van for mobile pet grooming."

"Sounds interesting." Kevin opened a case of water and began putting bottles on ice. "But l have a lucrative job opportunity for you to consider."

"I'm listening."

"Jack Broms, a foreman I've worked for, called me."

"I know Jack." Pete arranged liter bottles of various types of soft drinks.

"Yeah? Well, he's working on a rig off the Louisiana coast and had two of his crew back out at the last minute—health and family issues. I've signed on, and he asked me to recruit another worker."

Pete wanted to be free to resume the house restoration as soon as he got the go-ahead from Marigold and Petunia but asked anyhow. "What's the start-up date?"

"That's the downside. We leave tomorrow and will be gone an extended period—could be two months or more. Any chance you could put your project on hold for a while and join me?"

Pete shook his head. "That wouldn't work."

"I understand, but don't be too hasty to turn down the offer. Remember, there's a handsome bonus paid when you have to leave on short notice. Think on it."

"Right." Pete positioned cups and ice.

"Looks like another shuttle just arrived. I'm going to mingle for a few," Kevin said. "I'll be back to relieve you shortly." Kevin grabbed a water and joined a group finding seats at one of the tables.

A flash of red coming into the banquet room caught Pete's eye. Kali. She sauntered across the banquet room and slid onto a stool in front of him. She presented a striking image in a red, strapless, knee-length dress. Her long, thick, blonde hair hung smooth and straight, touching her bare shoulders.

"Hi, Pete. Fix me a Coke, lots of ice, will you?"

"I thought you'd be manning the registration table," Pete said.

"They have plenty of help."

"Any of your cheerleading girlfriends going to make it this time?" Kali was the only one who still lived in Hamilton Harbor.

"Doubtful. You wouldn't find me here if I could move somewhere with more opportunity." She scanned the room. "Seen Lyman?"

"Not yet."

Why would she be looking for Lyman to pal with? She took a sip of her drink, then ran her index finger, sporting a red manicured fingernail, around the rim of the cup. The color matched the red Claudia had on her nails when he fished her out of the bushes. Pete's stomach lurched. Was Kali trying to make a clone of Claudia?

"Speak of the proverbial devil," Pete said.

Lyman entered the room with a swagger. He tipped his hat to anyone who looked his way, making his arrival hard to miss.

"Hey, Lyman," Bill Graves, former center on the football team, called out. "Just letting you know I'm keeping my closet locked tight. Don't want you finding any of my skeletons." His comment raised laughter from the group talking to Graves.

"I might just stop by and rattle that lock, old buddy. Grabber headlines is the name of the game."

Kali waved Lyman to the drink table. "Hi, I've been looking for you." Kali spoke to Lyman and then Pete. "Lyman's going to cover the van dedication Sunday."

Pete's jaw tensed. Lyman used to run track but discovered he was better at running his mouth than running the 800-meter. "Think you can stick to the facts?"

Lyman tugged at his collar. "Of course. Got any root beer?"

Kali stepped away to speak to the old football coach.

Pete poured the drink for Lyman. "You *are* working on that front-page, follow-up story on Claudia we talked about?" Pete asked, eyebrow raised.

Lyman nodded. "I've got it all planned." He took the drink and sucked the foam off the top.

"Why write such a damaging headline in the first place?"

Lyman shrugged. "Sells papers. Gets people talking."

"Well, get people talking about the good Claudia's doing in the community, finding homes for shelter dogs."

"Sure. Sure thing."

Kevin and Kali returned.

Kali hooked Lyman's arm. "Let's go where we can talk." She steered him toward the stage beside the buffet table.

"I've got things covered here," Kevin said. "Go get something to eat."

Pete went to the buffet and had trouble concentrating on food selections. Lyman tripped and fell against the sound board as he stepped up on the stage behind Kali. What was Kali up to that she needed to talk to Lyman in private?

"Any chance you can forget writing a follow-up article on Claudia? Why beat a dead horse?"

Pete had started to pick up a sandwich but stopped mid-reach. He'd heard Kali as if she were standing next to him. Clearly. Lyman must have activated the sound on the PA system. The volume was low, but he could hear everything they were saying from his vantage point.

"Because a certain guy named Pete would mess up this good-lookin' nose of mine. I need it for snooping—my livelihood, you know."

At least Lyman had understood Pete's non-verbal communication over the article retraction.

"What about *my* livelihood?" Kali broadcasted. "I just convinced Claudia to leave here. I need her to go to Birmingham with me. When you found out about her arrest, that article was the perfect push."

Pete set down his plate. A few of the others in the room looked at the stage.

"Look, Kali. Pete's enamored with this girl. I promised I'd do a positive article on her," Lyman said. "That shouldn't stop her from going to Birmingham with you."

People stopped talking.

"Hey, Pete, you enamored again?" Bill Graves called out to him.

Lyman and Kali turned to face the group.

"I thought you got cured of that amorous ailment in high school," Bill teased. Laughter tittered through the gathering.

Pete's stomach tightened.

"What's this, Lyman? Are you starting an alumni gossip promotion?" Marvin Rhodes, former baseball star, asked.

Lyman's brow furrowed. "What are you talking about?"

"Don't tell me you didn't know you had the microphone on." Rhodes said.

Kali laughed—just as she had when he'd asked her for a date in high school—only this time the laugh was amplified throughout the room.

"Sure. Just a gag. A little preview of Lyman's new tell-all." Kali said.

"Oh … yeah." Lyman chimed in. "Watch for the column, and I'll be depending on all of you for material."

"So, Pete. Are you and the dog groomer an item?" Bill asked.

More laughter spread throughout the room. Pete managed a half smile.

His head reeled. Claudia was leaving. What about the mobile unit he'd just outfitted for her? He'd been picturing her surprise since the moment he'd started. How could she leave when so many were counting on her? She'd been around Kali too long.

Claudia had knocked him off his feet in more ways than one. Working with her, finding the secret room, the kiss. She was perfect just as she was, but she didn't believe it. And now she was leaving? Would she really walk out on her mobile grooming service? His chest constricted, and a heat crept up his neck to his tightened jaw. His spirit stirred. Remaining quiet was not an option. People in the room had resumed some conversation but it came to a halt when Pete moved closer to the stage. He had to speak up.

"Kali. You've been trying to change Claudia to suit your purposes and using Lyman to boost your agenda. But why? You've got enough talent in your little finger to sell a piece of swamp land as a tropical oasis. You don't need to use Claudia and create your own supporter to accomplish what you want."

He shifted eye contact and surged ahead before he could talk himself out of saying more. "And Lyman, you have tremendous potential for putting words together creatively for eye-popping headlines. Why not use that talent for good instead of hurting people?"

Pete waved his hands in a sweeping gesture. "All of us here know and accept both of you as you are."

His words got a "sure do" response and nods from the onlookers. Lyman adjusted his hat. Kali tugged a strand of hair behind her ear and lowered her head.

Pete continued. "Be yourself and let others do the same. If Claudia really wants the changes you've encouraged, Kali, and decides it's best to move to Birmingham, that's one thing. But not if it's due to some devious scheme."

Suddenly aware of the stilled room and gaping stares, Pete halted and tugged at his collar. "Sorry ... I ... sorry." He jammed his hands into his pockets, turned on his heel, and strode back to the drink table. Chatter erupted about the room.

"Hey, you gave them what for," Kevin said. "I didn't know you had it in you."

"Me either." Pete's breath came in short spurts. His mouth dry, he jerked a water bottle from the cooler, unscrewed the cap and drained half of it, allowing the liquid to cool his throat. He slumped against the wall behind the drink station. He stared at the linoleum tiles beneath his feet, like the ones he'd been ripping out at the Hamilton house.

"No matter. About your job offer, what time is the crew leaving?"

Claudia knocked on Francine's door at The Top of the Harbor. A cheery grapevine wreath with pink flowers and a little plaque that read, "A Merry Heart Doeth Good Like a Medicine," accented the door. She could use a merry heart.

She attempted to wipe the nervousness from her hands onto her shorts. Just as she did seventeen years ago. So many years had passed since losing her parents—and now to have their photo returned defied description.

It seemed like yesterday when she sat in Gramma's living room and stared at the white cast on her leg. Her broken ankle had ached but nothing like her heart.

She toyed with the rough-textured, hand-crocheted doilies pinned to the arms of the upholstered chair, while the investigator spoke to Gramma. "Part of the boat's hull was discovered and two life rings. At this time, all those on board are presumed lost."

Lost people can be found. "I'll give you a picture of my parents," she'd blurted. "Maybe someone will find them."

"A picture would be very helpful."

Claudia maneuvered the knee scooter into the guest room—her room while her parents were on their anniversary cruise. She grabbed the picture and scooted back to the living room.

"Here." She'd wanted to be useful. Helpful. Instead of the reason her parents left the cruise ship when she broke her ankle. The reason they were on the small craft. The reason they were swallowed up by the deep. The kind eyes of the investigator as he accepted the picture helped curb some of her guilt. The officer's folder closed over her parents' faces—the last remembrance she had of them.

Francine opened the door.

"Come in. Come in." She motioned Claudia into the cheerful apartment that spoke of cozy comfort and smelled of lemon-scented furniture polish.

"Toby, your teacher is here." Toby maintained his nonchalant air and sat dutifully at Francine's feet.

"Hi, Toby. You were one of my star pupils."

Toby waggled his stump and went to lay down under the dark-wood coffee table, polished to a high sheen.

"I'm so excited Lake was able to get your photo," Francine said. "He explained closed cases are generally marked for destruction after so many years. But this case, lost at sea, well …"

"Was never closed?"

"I guess not, officially. Please, have a seat."

Claudia sank into the puffy upholstered couch while Francine retrieved a tan clasp envelope from her desk.

"Here you are, dear. Would you like to be alone?"

"No. Oh, no. Please, I want you to see the picture."

Claudia's hands trembled as she accepted the envelope. Resting the envelope on her lap, she pushed up the sides of the metal clasp, lifted the flap and tugged at the picture, sliding it out slowly. Her dad, his hair thick and curly, and her mom with silky smooth red hair. They held hands, their heads touching.

Claudia wiped at a tear trickling down her cheek.

"Here you go." Francine handed her a tissue and sat beside her.

Claudia dabbed at her eyes. "Thank you. She turned the photo for Francine to see. "I remember when the picture was taken. My mom's friend was practicing for a photography class. They're sitting on our back-porch swing." Claudia pointed. "That's the playhouse Daddy built for me."

"Oh my. Such a lovely couple."

Claudia turned the photo over. "Could I see your Bible? My mother wrote some verses on the back when she gave me this picture."

"Of course. It's on the side table next to you on top of my journal."

"Do you keep a Bible study journal?"

"I do. This is my morning study spot."

"My mother did her Bible study and journaling at the kitchen table. I've started doing the same."

"Valuable time."

Claudia opened Francine's Bible to Ephesians 2:10 and read out loud, "For we are … his workmanship." Her throat closed, and her voice cracked. Tears welled and from somewhere deep inside, she sobbed. She felt another tissue poked in her hand and a comforting touch on her shoulder. Francine remained close but silent. After a moment, Claudia sniffed and blew her nose. "I'm sorry to go all to pieces on you."

"No need to apologize." Francine patted her shoulder. "Scripture has a way of reaching down and speaking to the heart."

"I told my mother I was a freak."

"Why would you call yourself a freak?"

Claudia lifted her hands. "Suitable for a professional basketball player." She pointed down. "And size thirteen feet. I accused my mother of creating a freak." She snuffled. "She gave me this Scripture, and I never even bothered to look it up."

"Would you like me to read it?"

"Please." Claudia handed her the Bible.

"For we are his workmanship, created in Christ Jesus unto good works, which God hath before ordained that we should walk in them." She laid the Bible in her lap. "Your mother knew, and God knew, you would need this Scripture."

"You think so?" Claudia wiped at her eyes with the heels of her hands. "Because I'm in a quandary now about where these big feet should be walking. Kali is encouraging me to go with her to Birmingham and work for Sterling. That would get me away from this terrible dog theft publicity. But then there's Elaine and all of you at the church ... and Pete." Why did she even mention him? "But I don't think he'd care."

"Hmm. Yes, Pete, a good, hard-working man." Francine said. "They don't come any better than him."

"Right. And a man of few words." What Francine said about Pete was true. How could she think Pete leaked information about her to a newspaper reporter?

"And don't forget the van donation." Francine continued.

"The van, which I can use, belongs to the church. Kali says Sterling would provide a van for me in Birmingham. Since the publication of that awful news article and all the cancellations at the grooming shop, I'm wondering if I should leave."

Francine chuckled. "Listen. Let me share a saying I heard my husband quote many times. 'Those that mind, don't matter, and those that matter, don't mind.' Things like false dog theft charges and big hands and feet matter less than the size of your heart. And it's your heart that you need to follow. I'm praying for you, dear." Francine selected a bookmark from her Bible. "Add these Scriptures to those from your mother. Go to sleep with the truths of these Scriptures on your heart, and I believe God will give you the answer you're seeking."

Chapter 17

Pete didn't feel like talking. The eight-man crew gathered around the outside tables of the marina snack bar to await the boat captain's signal for departure. They caught up on the latest news and spun tales of shore leave as squealing seagulls swooped down for bits of discarded bread or salty fries.

Pete gazed at the cheerless gray clouds that hung low on the summer horizon and avoided talking. Socializing was never his strong suit. He'd always found a certain satisfaction in being alone. But not today. Leaning on the dock rail, out of earshot of the others, only left him sad and empty.

Pete shoved his hands in his jeans pockets and descended the stairs that led to the beach. The sand under his rubber-soled shoes squeaked soft protests as he ambled to the water's edge. He picked up a partially exposed sand dollar in the wet sand. It was broken, cold, and hard. If it were whole, it would carry value—broken, it was worthless. He flung it like a Frisbee into the lapping waves.

Earlier, when he had adjusted Francine's cabinet door, she had said, "You're a man running from love."

When she handed him one of her bookmarks, he'd asked, "Why would you say that?"

"Claudia is thinking she might need to leave town but wishes for a reason to stay. When Lidia left you, it was for selfish reasons. It's obvious you care about Claudia, yet your pride stands in the way.

Pete hung his head. "You know the saying. Fool me once shame on you. Fool me twice, shame on me."

"Has Claudia fooled you?"

"Well, ... no."

"Are all men alike?"

"Not at all."

"Why would you think all women are alike?"

Why? Experience. His father had warned him. You get too close to a woman, you set yourself up for hurt. He didn't want to go through unlucky-in-love incidents like his dad. "I need to stick to work. With the Hamilton sisters delaying the restoration, I couldn't pass up the oil rig opportunity."

Pete fingered the construction paper bookmark in his pocket. He didn't need to reread it. He had it memorized. "*The Lord God said, "It is not good for the man to be alone. I will make a helper suitable for him. Genesis 2:18"*

Francine meant well.

The clatter of a lone hermit crab making its way across a discarded drink can captured Pete's attention. Could the creature be content in his solitude? Was he isolated by choice or circumstances he couldn't control?

Across the bay, he could see the pass—the deep-water gateway to endless waters that carried its own vast range of emotions—calm yet stormy, peaceful yet hostile. Rippling water inched its way upward then back on the rock barrier that separated the bay from the open Gulf. The tide was on the rise.

In Pete's experience, the sea with its ceaseless motion could grasp problems and roll them into nonexistence. The image of Claudia disappointing the seniors, his desire to hold her ... kiss her, could be swallowed and eradicated in the swelling waters. He would find peace in the steady purring of engines driving pipe deep below the surface of the Gulf.

Heavy booted steps thudded out a swift rhythmic pace on the boat dock behind him.

"Hey, Cullen! You better be making your way back. We'll be leaving as soon as we finish refueling."

The call from the boat captain accentuated the finality and purpose of the moment.

Claudia riveted her gaze on the illumined cross hanging high above the stage in New Hope Community Church. She knelt on the soft cushion at the altar. The treasured envelope holding her parents' photo lay on her left. Clover at her side seemed at home in the quiet of the sanctuary.

She'd tried to follow Francine's instructions to pray and sleep with the truths of Scripture on her heart but did little sleeping. Claudia rolled her shoulders to ease the tension in her neck. The solitude of the church, bustling with song and a sermon earlier that day, stilled her spirit.

She slid Francine's bookmark and the photo of her parents from the envelope. Mama and Daddy, the perfect couple. Though reduced to one dimension on photo paper, their images wrapped her with a sense of contentment, like a security blanket lost and found.

Turning the photo over, she touched the Scripture in her mother's handwriting. The connection took her back to nighttime prayers huddled with her mom and dad at her bedside. She studied the Scriptures from her mother and Francine's bookmarks. The words declared that she was God's workmanship created to do good works, and she could do all things with Christ's strength.

One verse from Francine reminded her that all things work together for good to them that love God. Good could come from her parents' death? Could the devastating article Lyman wrote somehow work for good? Was the negative publicity a sign she should go to Birmingham? She touched the clover at her neck. Was she attaching more significance to the charm than she should? She was Kali's friend, not her good luck. Pete had made her see that.

Gramma and Kali had tried to change her image. But was this the change God wanted? Pete said God had plans for her as she was, not as someone else wanted her to be. She ran her thumb over the Ephesians Scripture. Was she really God's workmanship?

"Lord, I want to know your direction for me, just as I am," she whispered.

She peered into the old theatre orchestra pit. Its darkness reminded her of the depths that swallowed her parents and held them captive forever. But out of this pit this morning came the brilliance of music that held the power to lift the soul to new heights.

Psalm 91:1 had been written on the wall in the hidden room. Claudia flipped pages in the Bible at the altar, then read. "He that dwelleth in the secret place of the most High, shall abide under the shadow of the Almighty." She raised her eyes again to the backlit cross. Her parents weren't held in a never-ending hole. They were with Jesus. She held the photo to her heart and breathed deeply. "Lord," she whispered, "I release the pain of my parents' death to you."

Clover shifted and rested his chin on her ankle. She stilled and let the memory of experiencing the secret place with Pete envelop her. That shared time had brought her to a place of comfort and security—a place her soul could call home.

The longer she remained in silence, the weightier the little clover from Kali became around her neck. "Lord I want to follow your plan, not someone else's." She reached behind her neck, unhooked the clasp to the necklace, and laid it on the altar. Her shoulders straightened as if she had just shrugged off a twenty-five-pound backpack. Her whole body relaxed.

She wished she could talk to her mom and dad again, but at least she could feel the blessing of their love and sweet memories they left behind. Claudia smiled at their photo through tears of remembrance—tears of release.

She grabbed a tissue from the altar, blew her nose, and wiped her eyes. Replacing the photo in the envelope and the bookmark in her dress pocket, she told Clover, "It's time we went to the van dedication."

Clover stood, ears perked and wagged his tail highlighting the brown splotch on his back.

Claudia stared at him.

"How did I miss it?"

Clover tilted his head and stared back at her.

"A heart."

Claudia ran her finger along the soft fur design on Clover's backside.

"Clover, buddy, we've got to find Pete and tell him ... I see the heart."

Chapter 18

Claudia, a new spring in her step, hurried from the sanctuary with Clover at her side. Several church members were gathering in the parking lot for the van dedication. Kali stood alongside Mr. Sterling. Izzie and Emme from The Flower Cottage were there with Richie and Emme's husband, Clifton. Olivia, the bichon brothers, Aunt Lucy, Francine, Dave, Elaine and her girls chatted with one another.

"Hello, all," Claudia said. She embraced her aunt, squeezed Francine's hand, and greeted the others.

Jeff arrived in his patrol car. "Is this a lawful gathering?"

"Best keep an eye on us, so we don't get out of hand," Dave said.

"I believe I will." Jeff parked and joined the group.

Where was Pete?

Pastor Creighton began his remarks, "We are gathered in special thanks for the kindness shown to our church fellowship with an extraordinary gift. This van will be used to provide aid to our elder population with the unique added feature of pet therapy and grooming. Today, we dedicate this van to the Lord's service. Mr. Sterling, if you would come forward."

Mr. Sterling stepped beside the white van lettered with *Helping Hands Ministry, New Hope Community Church*. His voice had no need for amplification.

"Folks, I may live in Birmingham, but I have a vacation home here in Hamilton Harbor and feel a special attachment to your community. I have been especially blessed in recent weeks by a certain person in your church community who helped me train my little dog, Bitsy. Where's Claudia Stewart?"

Jeff and Elaine pointed to Claudia. She could feel her face flush with all eyes on her.

"Come up here. No time to be shy." Mr. Sterling motioned her to come forward with the vigor of a policeman directing traffic.

"I learned from Ms. Reppen," he nodded toward Kali, "that this young lady had a dream of taking her grooming services to those who couldn't handle pet care on their own. I'd thought I might recruit this lady to bring her good work to Birmingham, but from the mutual caring shared here today, I can see why she might not want to leave. So, with no further fuss, it is my privilege to present this van for use in your Helping Hands Ministry for mobile pet grooming and other ministry needs as you see fit."

Cheers and applause erupted. Francine caught Claudia's eye and nodded with a firmness that said she'd been given the answer to her prayer for direction.

Mr. Sterling held up both hands and in a raised voice said, "I also want to acknowledge someone else, Pete Cullen, who outfitted the interior. Is he here?"

Pete outfitted the van? When did he have time to work on the van? Claudia scanned the group. No Pete.

Mr. Sterling continued, "Well, when you see him, let him know you appreciate him. I understand he put in many late-night hours to get the van ready for today's presentation." He held up a set of keys and pressed the remote button. The side door rumbled open. "And now it is with great pleasure, Pastor Creighton, I hand these keys over to you and New Hope Community Church."

After more clapping, the gathering began milling around. Some went to speak to Mr. Sterling, others stepped into the van for a look.

Olivia Appleberry, instead of being pulled by Corky and Fritz on their double leash, approached Claudia with the dogs walking alongside her. "Claudia, your suggestion for two separate leashes is worth way more than that van donation—to me anyhow. I can never repay you."

"Your thanks is all the payment I need."

"Well, you've got that." She rolled disapproving eyes toward Lyman. "And I'm telling everyone I know what hogwash that article was about you being a dog thief." She raised her hand and waved. "Excuse me. There's someone I need to tell right now."

Claudia joined Francine who was talking to Kali. "Thank you. Without your telling Mr. Sterling about Claudia's mobile grooming idea, this van donation wouldn't have happened," Francine said.

"You are very welcome. But I just happened to overhear Pete telling Elaine that Claudia wanted to offer mobile grooming. My part was extremely minor."

"Minor parts are important too. Excuse me, I want to speak to Mr. Sterling."

Kali turned to Claudia. "I do hope this helps fulfill your dream." She spoke with a sincerity she'd not heard from Kali before. "Listen, I know I pushed you into that dog class, but everything turned out well."

Claudia nodded. "It has turned out well, and Mr. Sterling is right. I have found a home here."

"I can see that. So, forget my push to move to Birmingham. I thought we had to be a package deal for Sterling, but it turns out he still wants me in Birmingham for my sales skills."

"That's great." Claudia hugged Kali. Clover put his paw on Kali's high-spiked shoe. And wagged his tail.

"Look at that." Kali slowly reached down, showing Clover the back of her hand. He sniffed and wagged. Kali gingerly patted his head. No growling. "Good boy. Is all forgiven?" She looked at Claudia. "Do you think he knew I wanted you to move?"

Claudia smiled. "Maybe."

"It's obvious you've found your niche here, and goodness knows, Pete doesn't want you to leave."

"Why would you say that? He's not even here."

"Are you kidding? I wish he looked at me like he does you. I've known him a long time. He's a tough one to figure, and once he's wounded—"

Lyman walked up. "Who's wounded?"

"Tell Claudia about the retraction you're printing on Pete's insistence," Kali said.

"Pete's insistence?" Claudia turned to Lyman.

Lyman nodded and pointed to his nose. "I wanted to keep this beaut intact. Don't worry. I have a follow-up headliner that you were cleared of wrongdoing. Nothing personal, by the way, on the article I wrote. I sniff out the interesting angles and that was—"

Clover grumbled.

"Made to order?" Claudia stooped down to pet Clover.

"Yeah. I guess so."

"Story of my life," Claudia said. "A black—"

"Don't say it. Come with me," Elaine interrupted, and Aunt Lucy took Claudia's elbow to steer her in the direction of the van. "You need to look inside this van."

When Claudia stepped into the interior, her chest tingled and she gasped. Hues of bright yellow, hot pink, and vibrant green leaped out to greet her. The colors highlighted two framed and stacked kennels, a grooming table, an elevated tub in the rear, and storage racks that lined the vacant space behind the driver and passenger seats.

"These colors pop," Izzie said. Her silver dangling earrings reflected off the dome light of the van and spotlighted Pete's handiwork.

Paw prints, just like those Pete and she had created in her shop, meandered across the interior shelving. Small painted lettering on the trim under the grooming table read *Some of God's Miracles Come with Paws*.

"That boy sure does nice work, don't you think?" Dave's comment stung the air.

Like water rising to flood stage, tears brimmed in Claudia's eyes. Her voice caught, "I ... uh, think ... yes."

She managed to squeeze out the "yes" in a hushed tone.

Where was Pete? He'd shared her desire for a mobile unit, demanded Lyman do a follow-up story on her, and worked late nights on the van for her, and he wasn't even here?

She ran her hand over the acrylic painted paw prints. The memory of working with him, his touch whenever she fell ... his kiss, all flooded her soul.

Claudia stepped down from the van, and Clover hopped down next to her. Aunt Lucy shoved a tissue into her hand. Elaine materialized next to them.

"I don't understand why Pete's not here," Claudia said.

"I can't say it surprises me too much," Elaine said. "He hates to be the center of attention. Here, he gave me this to give to you today."

Claudia wrinkled her forehead and took the plain white envelope from Elaine's outstretched hand. She broke the seal, slipped the note out, and read.

I'm returning for a stint on the oil rigs and won't make the dedication. I hope the van interior suits your needs. The idea of mobile dog grooming should serve you well in Birmingham. I pray God's best for you. Pete.

Claudia slowly refolded the note. A wayward tear dropped on the paper as she slid it back in the envelope.

Kali walked up. "What do you think of Pete's work?"

Claudia stared at Kali and held up the envelope "Pete wishes me well in Birmingham. He's going back on the oil rigs. Why does he think I'm going to Birmingham?"

"The oil rigs?" Kali raised her eyebrows. "I saw him talking to Kevin, who works on the oil rigs, at the reunion last night."

"Wait a minute. In high school. Cheerleader. Laughing at Pete. Was that you?"

"He told you? I'm afraid I'm guilty as charged. And I'm afraid he knew about Birmingham, because ... I thought I had you convinced to go." The intensity of Kali's words slowed then picked up. "Hold up. He thinks you're leaving. So, he's leaving."

"But why? He's got the house he's working on."

Kali threw her hands up. "Do I have to spell it out for you? Pete's in love with you and won't admit it."

"Pete, in love with me? He won't even speak to me."

"And to top that off, you're in love with him and don't seem to know it."

"In love with him?"

"She's right," Aunt Lucy said, emphasizing the "right."

Lyman entered himself into the conversation. "Can I pick 'em or what? Why else would he come unglued and defend your honor?"

Aunt Lucy leaned in to comment. "It's a sign of true love, when a man sacrifices for you and doesn't want to see you hurt."

Claudia teared up again. The little group expanded to include Dave, Francine, and Jeff. Elaine spoke. "Aunt Lucy is spot-on."

"But—"

"It was written all over him when he handed me that letter to give you," Elaine said.

Francine said, "I saw the I-love-her-but-will-sacrifice-my-feelings-in-order-for-her-to-be-happy look when he came by my apartment to say good-bye."

"And I saw the I-gotta-get-away-or-my-heart-will-break look when he finished the van and asked me to drive it over here," Dave added. "He told me he was meeting the crew shuttle that leaves from the marina at five." He rocked forward on his feet. "I could call Joe at the marina and tell him to take his time refueling that crew boat." The corners of his mouth raised in a conspiratorial grin.

Claudia looked from one face to the next. She saw love and caring concern in action.

"I say we get this girl down to the Bayside Marina, ASAP," Jeff said.

"Are you serious?" Claudia asked.

"As a jail escape."

"Do you really think I should go after him?" Did she say that? Was she an actor playing a part in a scene?

"Do you love him?" Elaine asked.

"Well, I care for him ... a lot," she heard herself answer.

"Then I think you've found your Prince Charming," Elaine said.

She looked at Kali who raised her shoulders and hands. "If I had a guy who stood up for me like he does you, I wouldn't be letting him get away."

Pete loved her? From the feelings radiating from her heart, she did love Pete. Feelings sparked the moment she knocked him off that ladder—the first time.

"Can I get there in time?" Claudia asked.

Dave looked at his watch, "I don't know how long Joe will be able to hold that boat."

"It's a thirty-five-minute drive, about half that with blue lights and siren," Jeff said.

"You better get moving then. Joe told me Captain Orn didn't want to be late meeting the oil rig transport. I know that captain. Once he leaves the dock, there's no turning back."

"Okay. Elaine, Claudia, get in the patrol car. Ms. Francine, please take the girls to their class. Aunt Lucy, you take Clover." Jeff barked out instructions as if he were heading up a criminal investigation.

Everyone buzzed around Claudia reciting their lines in this strange scene. Aunt Lucy took Clover's leash. Jeff placed a firm hand on Claudia's back, steering her to the police cruiser. Aunt Lucy and Elaine followed.

"I'd join the fun, but I have to leave with Mr. Sterling," Kali said.

"I'll let them know you're on the way." Dave punched numbers into his cell phone.

"Go in the patrol car? Can I do that?" Claudia asked as she tried to grasp all that was happening.

"You can on Jeff's orders," Elaine said.

Aunt Lucy patted Claudia's shoulder and opened the police car passenger door. "I'll get Clover back to the shop for you." Claudia caught the comforting scent of witch hazel as Aunt Lucy's soft cheek brushed against her own. She embraced her aunt.

"Do you think Mom and Dad would have approved of me chasing after a guy?"

"I do, if the guy was Pete. Now go after him," Aunt Lucy said and closed the door with a decisive push.

Elaine got in the back seat. Seagulls cheered overhead.

Jeff keyed his radio. "Eight to base."

"Go ahead eight," the radio operator responded.

"10-51, 10-18 to the fuel docks. Citizen 10-12 for a 10-33 contact with a crew member disembarking from the Bayside Marina."

"10-26. Be careful."

Claudia turned to Elaine with a wrinkled brow. "He's just telling the radio operator he's en route, blue lights and siren, with a citizen on an emergency," Elaine said.

Claudia was sucked in a whirlwind, the whole idea dizzying. The anvil weighing on her heart these last weeks without Pete seemed to be lifted at the very idea of going after him.

Jeff turned the key in the ignition and flipped a switch. Rays of blue lights swirled. The siren whined. The car started moving, but Claudia had the distinct feeling they were getting a boost from another power. The power of one who says we are his workmanship. The power written about on the back of her parents' photo.

Pete boarded the transport boat that would take him away from concerns on land. On the steel oil rig platform a hundred twenty-five miles out, he could be anonymous. He had buried troubles out there before. He could do it again. The vastness of the ocean and its creator would make his problems seem small in comparison and evaporate in the breeze.

The inboard engines thundered into action, and the boat started moving. He was barely aware of his crewmates trying to make their opinions known about the latest trades in the Atlanta Braves and Mariners baseball teams. Pete used to follow the major leagues but not this year.

Catching up on the world of team standings and statistics would be something to occupy his mind. He had to have something to replace the thoughts of Claudia that kept creeping into his head. Like water finding its way through a breach in a dam wall, he'd plug the hole with baseball. The boat motors picked up speed. Pete settled on a section of the cracked vinyl bench seat in the cabin's interior and began listening to the sports chatter.

"The Braves traded him so they could afford to get a good short stop and a new pitcher."

"Whatever the reason, I think they made a lousy trade."

Only minutes away from the dock and his baseball interest waned. What happened at the dedication? Did Claudia like the way he outfitted the van? Claudia again. He left the cabin and stepped to the railing of the crew shuttle. The sun reached its long summer rays over the bay waters. He closed his eyes and inhaled the salty air. Events of the previous night replayed—learning Claudia was leaving and the broadcasting of his interest in her.

He needed to get away. To stop dwelling on his disappointment and think on things that were praiseworthy. He could be thankful for this oil rig job and praise God for his ability to work and help others. Was this his calling? Was being single the state to which he should be content? *Lord, in these next weeks, please help me accept and sort out my feelings*

Chapter 19

"You're too late. The boat left five minutes ago."

Jeff, Elaine, and Claudia stood by the empty docking area where boats refueled. The strong gasoline fumes lingered in the air. Claudia's chest constricted closing in on her heart. Her fear of the treacherous water battled with the pain of not being able to tell Pete she cared for him. She stood helpless, numb.

The departing vessel plowed through the choppy waters, carrying Pete out to sea. She couldn't watch and, instead, focused on the rolling swells lapping against the barnacle encrusted pilings.

"You the ones I was holding the boat for?"

"We are," Jeff said.

"Dave said it was a heart matter?"

"Right." Jeff ran his fingers through his hair.

"I stalled as long as I could, but Captain Orn complained of a deadline. I couldn't hold him any longer."

"Do you have radio communication with them?" Jeff asked.

"Not me." With a wink of a sun-crinkled eye, Joe squeezed on a lump of chewing tobacco that puffed out his cheek, puckered his lips, and skillfully shot a coffee-colored stream of spit into a five-gallon bucket on the dock's edge.

"Isn't there anything we can do?" Elaine said.

Claudia lifted her gaze and saw the transport continue to inch its way toward the pass that would put Pete in the Gulf. *Lord, show us a way.*

"You folks want to catch that boat?" A man hosing down the deck of a deep-sea fishing boat called to them. A small sign hanging over the boat cabin read: *Capt. J.C. Lewis.*

The little gathering moved closer to his boat.

"Think you could catch up with 'em, J.C.?" Joe asked.

J.C. chewed on an unlit cigar. He pinched it between his teeth, turned, and squinted at the boat. "Does a cat have a passin' gear?"

"We need to get her to that boat," Jeff said, putting his hand on Claudia's back.

Was Jeff suggesting she ride on a watercraft? Claudia's heartbeat raced. Sound seemed to come from far away. Her knees went weak.

Captain Lewis gave the receding ship a calculated look. "I can overtake her in my skiff," he said with confidence. "Joe here said it's something about a heart? Somebody sick?"

"It's a matter of ... you know," Elaine cupped her hands and placed them over her heart and looked at Claudia, "the heart."

J.C. used his lips to maneuver his cigar over to one side of his mouth and flashed a wide grin exposing perfectly shaped dentures. "Oh."

"He'll be gone at least two months," Elaine said nodding toward the boat in the bay.

Two months. Blood drained from Claudia's face, leaving her dizzy. Maybe time apart would be a good thing. Who was she kidding? Time apart from Pete is what she had now, and she was miserable. But the water. Getting on a boat. Her throat closed. She squeaked. "I can't wait two months."

"Understood." J.C., a man with beef-jerky-like skin and eyes that hinted at a joyful heart, formed his words around his cigar. "I'll get you there, little lady. No charge. Just filled 'er up this mornin'. All we gotta do is untie and let 'er rip."

Claudia met the questioning gaze of Elaine—the one person there who understood her fear of water. "Can you do it?" she asked.

Could she? Claudia summoned the words on the bookmark given to her by Francine about being able to do all things. *Lord, if this is you, give me strength.* In him, she could do this. She *would* do this. "Yes," she said and turned to give Elaine and Jeff a hug.

"Ready, little lady? No time to lose."

"I'm Claudia." After shaking J.C.'s rough hand, she shoved her hand into her pocket. It brushed against the stiff paper of Francine's bookmark. "Yes, sir, I'm ready."

"Then follow me." He toggled down the dock with one unbending leg, yet Claudia had to move fast to keep up.

With each pounded step came liberation until she reached the end of the dock, where a small skiff bobbed on the water. A puff of wind graced her face like her father's touch, and unseen air currents carried her mother's encouraging words, setting her free.

J.C. scaled down the ladder to the little boat. "Give me your hand," J.C. called to Claudia. She wished she hadn't worn a dress but climbing into a boat hadn't exactly been on her agenda.

Agreeing to launch into the deep with this burly, cigar-chomping man she had never laid eyes on before had to be the Lord. *Lord, help me trust you with my fear … and forget about my dress.*

She grabbed J.C.'s rough hand, and like one of her happy unleashed clients, Claudia took a leap of faith onto the boat.

J.C. turned the starter. The boat motor jerked as if slapped, sputtered, and fell silent. Claudia's stomach lurched. What happened to her confidence?

The starter ground like a garbage disposal. The seagulls shrieked. Pete's boat diminished.

A wave of nausea threatened. She closed her eyes and tried to press the feeling down, but the queasiness crept upward with each rocking motion of the boat.

Lord, you didn't bring me this far to get sick in a boat that won't even go.

J.C. gave the starter cord another yank. The motor coughed, released a puff of black smoke mixed with the smell of gas and oil, and roared to life.

"It's gonna be a bumpy ride, little lady." He tossed her an orange vest. "Think you can handle it?" J.C. shouted over the rumble of the motor.

Claudia donned the lifejacket and grabbed the sides of her seat. "I'm ready."

J.C. pushed the throttle to full.

Salty spray and stinging wind refreshed Claudia's spirit, lifting her queasiness and dissolving her fear into the air.

Chapter 20

Pete closed his eyes and let the heat of the sun warm his chilly heart. The seagulls above even seemed to call out "heat, heat, heat." He found solace in the fact that in God's amazing creation even the seagulls could be orchestrated to speak hope. Maybe one day he'd even be able to pray for Claudia's success in Birmingham without misery interfering.

"I'm not interested in baseball right now, either," Kevin said. He came to stand by Pete at the ship's railing.

"I may follow the Major Leagues later but not today," Pete said.

"I understand." Kevin joined Pete in contemplative silence for a moment.

"Did you hear that?" Kevin asked. "Sounded like someone shouting."

"Seagulls begging for attention," Pete said.

"I don't know. Sounds like a person to me." Kevin walked past Pete toward the stern.

Pete wished he could clear his thoughts of Claudia, like hitting the delete button on a computer. He stepped to the rear of the boat, ready for diversion. The sea gulls' call now sounded like "Pete" instead of "heat."

"Pete, Pete." Even the birds sounded like Claudia. Pete looked to the sky and spotted two gulls gliding on a wind current. He had it bad. Not thinking about the redhead who'd managed to capture his heart was impossible.

Other crew members gathered. Did they hear what he did?

"Captain, hold up!" Kevin shouted, looking down at the starboard side of the boat across from Pete. "We've got company."

"Bet it's that pesky Marine Patrol running a pollution check," the captain shouted loud enough to be heard over the roar of the twin inboard motors. "I already have to make up the fifteen-minute fueling delay."

He slowed the engines to a humming idle.

Crew members moved in Kevin's direction.

A gruff voice called out, "You got a Pete Cullen on board?"

"Pete. You better get over here," Kevin said.

Who would want him? Had the Hamilton house burned? Dave gone into the hospital? He'd stepped into the Twilight Zone.

Pete's eyes widened when he saw the small skiff bobbing on the choppy water alongside them. *Claudia.* The sunlight caught in her windblown curls. She wore the sunflower dress—the one that snapped his heart strings and left him trying to tighten them ever since. What was she doing here?

"Pete!" Claudia called again and waved her arms.

Pete leaned over the railing, "What's going on?"

She stared at him a long moment, then said, "I couldn't let you go without thanking you."

"For what?" he called down to her.

"The van … the work you did …" her voice trailed off. All eyes were on her. Captain Orn climbed from the bridge. His boots pounded against the deck.

"You're welcome," Pete answered. His eyes locked with hers.

"Awww … thanks … you're welcome," J.C. boomed out the words. "You two gonna get together or what?"

"What's all this about?" Captain Orn barked. He gave a questioning look to the men standing by the railing, and their attention shifted to Pete. "I don't have time for—"

"It's a heart problem," J.C. shouted up to Captain Orn.

"Heart?"

"You know." J.C. cupped his hands over his heart, tilted his head up, and batted his eyes at the captain.

"Achh. I can't take much of those sentiments coming from you, J.C." Captain Orn turned and eyed Pete with all the love of a drill sergeant. "Cullen, take care of this heart matter and be quick about it."

J.C. took the lifejacket Claudia shed and guided her with his hand on her elbow to the bow of the skiff. He steadied her while Pete reached down to grab her hand. A choppy wave wedged in between the two boats, pulling them apart. Pete lost his footing and hung precariously over the edge. He clung fiercely to Claudia over the widening gap.

"Grab his feet," Kevin said to his buddies.

"Toss 'em a rope," Captain Orn directed.

Pete's arms strained to keep his grip on Claudia's arms. The gap narrowed. Pete yanked, and Claudia shot over the side. She fell against Pete. Pete fell against Kevin. All three crash-landed in a heap underneath the ladder leading to the upper deck. Pete hopped up. He helped untangle Kevin and Claudia, who scrambled to straighten her dress.

"Man, good reflexes!" Kevin said, brushing himself off.

"Do you always have to make such dramatic entrances?" Pete said.

"I'm so sorry. I just had to see you."

"You braved the water. Why?"

Kevin gave Pete an encouraging slap on the back, nudging him closer to Claudia still under the ladder.

Claudia kept her eyes fastened on Pete's and raised her chin.

The clover necklace, ever-present since Kali gave it to her, was gone. He raised his eyes in question.

"I'm not going to Birmingham."

"Why?"

"A certain loveable guy pointed out a heart on Clover's rump. I saw the heart today."

"You think I'm loveable?"

"I'd say guys who see hearts on dogs must be loveable. If not, I'd have never stepped in that boat to come after you. Besides, I don't intend to miss out on God's best."

The crew became background scenery in this strange play. He had the lead role but couldn't remember his lines.

The wind subsided. All the oxygen seemed to be sucked from the air. A lone seagull swooped down and lit on the railing.

"And what do you believe is God's best?"

She cast jeweled eyes on him. A flash of fear took him back to high school when he was laughed at. The men's eyes bore holes in him.

Kevin pushed Pete closer to Claudia, "She's talking about you, buddy."

Pete stared at her. The intense heat of the sun hanging low in afternoon sky added to his discomfort. Claudia wrinkled her forehead. "Think you're tough enough to deal with a ladder-disaster person like me?"

The crowd about him no longer existed.

"I wouldn't want you any other way. After all, I've survived three of your ladder calamities." He brushed his hand against her cheek.

"Are you going to kiss her or just stand there and gawk?" Captain Orn bellowed.

"Kiss her!" shouted the crew.

And he did.

Pete drew her close. He leaned down, and as his lips touched hers, you would have thought the crew's favorite team had just won the World Series. Cheers erupted with applause accented by high-fives.

With all apprehension gone underneath the ship's ladder, only joy and tenderness of the moment remained.

Epilogue

Six months later.

"Why would SWAT call on you for assistance?"

Lyman Beardsley poked his hand-held tape recorder under Claudia's nose.

Claudia hugged her arms around her middle. Why couldn't she stop shaking? Richie was safe. She was safe. The early spring morning air in Feldman Park wasn't that chilly. Her muscles were spent. Her knees shook. She needed to sit down.

"Ms. Stewart, can you tell us what happened?"

She didn't trust her voice. "T-Tony ... Officer Duncan will answer your questions."

"Claudia." Pete called to her, making his way through the press of newspaper and television reporters gathering.

"Pete." Relief overtaking, Claudia collapsed against him. The adrenalin surge that had helped her pull Richie from the abandoned well had left her weak.

"I saw Emme and Clifton with Richie," Pete said. "They told me what happened. Are you okay?"

Claudia nodded, but a shiver ran from her shoulders to her toes. Pete's strong arms saturated Claudia with comfort medicine, while Tony fielded questions.

"It appeared to be about a twelve-foot drop. To get the boy out," Tony said, "I needed a rescuer to go in headfirst."

"Why Ms. Stewart?" a reporter asked.

"I knew her at Florida State. She was a trapeze artist in the university circus and had the exact skills needed to anchor her feet on the rope ladder we used to lower in the hole.

Video flood lights bore down on Claudia and she winced.

"Let's go over here and sit down." Pete steered her to a park bench.

Claudia sat down and stared at the location Jeff was marking off with yellow tape next to the Feldman house. It was the same location where, months earlier, she had caught her foot on the well cover.

"Pete, it was so dark … and scary … like being buried alive." She shuddered involuntarily. "Richie was crying with gut-wrenching shrieks. My legs were cramping. He grabbed onto my arms, but half-way up, one of his hands slipped … I thought I was going to lose him." She took a shaky breath.

"It's okay, honey. It's over."

Claudia buried her face into the crook of Pete's shoulder, and tears came in sobs. The smell of his cologne sent a soothing wave over her tense muscles.

"You had such a stranglehold on his other hand, he'll have an imprint to treasure for days," Pete said and stroked her hair.

As Pete spoke, Emme and Clifton approached holding Richie. "An imprint we will all cherish," Emme said.

Richie held up his dirt-streaked hand. "I got the ball."

"You sure did." Claudia wiped her eyes with Pete's handkerchief.

"Show Miss Claudia what else you found," Emme said. Richie handed his mom the baseball, reached in his pocket, and produced a coin in his grimy outstretched palm.

Pete took a closer look. "A gold coin. This was in the bottom of the well?"

Clifton nodded. "He must have scooped it up with the baseball."

"An interesting find." Claudia examined the coin. "1907." She placed the coin back in Richie's hand, and gave his hand a gentle squeeze. "You must have fallen into a wishing well, Richie."

"I was wishing to get out," he said, then poked out his lower lip. Everyone chuckled.

"Me too," Claudia said.

Jeff walked up. "I've got the area marked off and contacted the city manager."

"What will he do?" Clifton asked.

"He's sending a work crew to reseal the well. The cover was likely dislodged when the city cleared the property donated by the Hamilton sisters for the running trail."

Tony joined them. "I asked the news media to give you some time and space." He adjusted his Hamilton Harbor Police Department cap and tousled Richie's hair. "Sorry our Big Brother pitch and catch practice got interrupted this morning."

Addressing the others, he said, "When he ran after that wild pitch," he shook his head, "I won't forget his cry for help—ever. Before I had a chance to call on the radio for assistance, Claudia appeared on the jogging trail."

"Praise God," Emme said. "It was a divine appointment. Claudia, you were specially made and put there to save Richie."

"My sentiments exactly when Tony called me for a rope ladder," Jeff said.

Claudia rubbed her sore hands over the rope-burns on her ankles and feet. "Finally, my big hands and feet are useful for something other than circus entertainment."

"I told you. You're perfect just the way you are, Mrs. Cullen-to-be," Pete murmured the words, tickling her ear, and sending an electric quiver through every inch of her body. Claudia gave Pete's hand a squeeze.

"Speaking of divine appointment," Tony said, "isn't there a wedding day rule about the groom not seeing the bride before the ceremony?"

"As a wedding florist, I see lots of couples abide by the not-seeing-each-other custom to add excitement and anticipation to the ceremony," Emme said. "But I think there's been enough pre-ceremony excitement. I vote they get a pass on that tradition."

A few hours later, in the dressing room of New Hope Community Church, Elaine used a curling iron to tame Claudia's curls into soft tendrils. "Shall I sing a chorus of 'I told you so' to the twenty-seven-year-old bride who thought her time was running out?"

"What's that supposed to mean?"

"Don't you remember? I told you Mr. Right would come along, and you haven't even made twenty-eight yet."

Claudia smoothed her floor-length wedding gown. "I don't think a matron of honor is supposed to have a smug attitude with the bride."

"Not just the bride, I need to gloat over the groom too."

"You're ganging up on us?"

"I told Pete that Marigold and Petunia would love his work. Now, he's the proud owner of the restored Hamilton house. Which, by the way, will become the castle complete with a playhouse for you and your Prince Charming, my lady." Elaine pinched the sides of her dress and curtsied.

"Okay. Okay. I concede, you were right."

"Thanks. And because of your gracious concession, I will let you borrow the bracelet I wore at my wedding."

"Thank you," Claudia slipped the bracelet onto her wrist. "My dress is new, the bracelet is borrowed, and Francine's bookmark is tucked into my bouquet for something blue." The scripture Francine selected for Claudia's wedding day came from Psalm 139:14—"for I am fearfully and wonderfully made."

"I promised to provide you with something old, and here I am." Aunt Lucy stepped forward wearing her springtime lavender dress.

Everyone laughed.

"You're not old. You've just been around a while," Claudia said.

"Then here's a little something that you'll consider old for sure—my mother's locket, and I want you to keep it." She handed the locket to Claudia, a golden rectangle with a delicately engraved floral design.

Claudia pressed the latch. "Oh my. Mother and Daddy's picture." She stood and embraced her aunt. "Thank you so much. Will you put it on me?"

Claudia looked in the mirror as her aunt fastened the locket. "Please guys, no more sentimental stuff or my eye makeup will be a disaster."

There was a rap at the door. It was Tony, who had volunteered to play the wedding music CDs. "It's 6:30. Elaine, you're on."

"See you down front." Elaine gave Claudia a final hug.

Bridal chorus music began.

"Okay, you two," Volunteer photographer Kali said. "Smile like you are bride and escort." Claudia laughed, and Aunt Lucy obliged with a wide grin and patted Claudia's arm crooked in hers.

At the back of the old theater-turned-sanctuary, Claudia took in the full view. The small group gathered to witness her marriage to Pete was the perfect size, for everyone had a front row seat. There were Dave and Francine, Emme and Clifton, who held Richie in his lap, Izzie, who helped design the white satin bow and magnolia decorations that sweetened the air. Next to her was Pete's high school friend, Kevin. Even Mr. Sterling, who'd made a special trip from Birmingham, was there.

Elaine reached the altar, joining Pastor Creighton and best man Jeff. Finally, Claudia looked at Pete. His eyes met hers in a sweet caress.

"Have you ever seen anything so lovely?" Claudia said to her aunt.

"Yep. You. Are you ready to march?"

"Ready."

With vows spoken, and a prayer of blessing given at the altar, Claudia stood. The toe of her shoe caught on the hem of her dress. She fell against Pete.

"Sorry."

"No worry," he whispered into her hair. "You can lean on me all you want."

"You may kiss your bride," Pastor said.

Pete obliged with a head-spinning, breath-taking, fabulous kiss that reached deep into her soul. She touched the locket at her neck, then wrapped her arms about Pete and kissed him back with a force that would have caused most to lose their balance. But Pete kept them both firmly in place.

As she took in the sweetness of his kiss and the full impact of the man—her husband—holding her, she felt safe and secure. Surrounded by old friends and new, Claudia had indeed stumbled upon her special knight and a place to call home.

Dear Reader,

Thank you for joining me for Claudia and Pete's story, second in the Hamilton Harbor Legacy series. This book has gone through its own evolution and revelations along with Claudia and Pete's experiencing self-acceptance.

I first wrote Claudia as Lynn, who was superstitious and believed the right match for her would come from horoscope suggestions. But she gradually morphed into clumsy Claudia who decided she was a misfit. I always saw Pete as a hard-working man who appeared gruff because he feared exposing his loving heart. I enjoyed sending them on their journey to discover God's best for them.

In Pete and Claudia's relationship, they discover true love is finding someone who loves you just as you are—faults and all. After all, God loves us just as we are and wants us to come to him with our fears, our doubts, and our questions and misconceptions.

What a comforting thought and blessing when someone comes into our life with that mentality. Something clicks, and you see beyond the outer fringes to the inner man or woman, judging them not on their mistakes or outward appearance but their inner character.

Thank goodness God has that power to look inside our hearts, and we can rest in that assurance when we mess up, have a bad day, trip over our feet, or knock people off ladders.

If you enjoyed this story, please post a review on Amazon. And I hope you will look for the upcoming story from the Hamilton Harbor coastal town where an interior design contest to save the homes on Feldman Square ends up revealing secrets from the past and valuable lessons in restoration, faith, and love.

I love to hear from readers. Contact me at www.sallyjopitts.com. In the meantime, enjoy this recipe for Aunt Lucy's Pot Roast.

AUNT LUCY'S POT ROAST

1 3 ½ - 4-lb beef arm or boneless pot roast
1 pkg dry onion soup
1 can cream of mushroom soup
3 carrots, pared and sliced in chunks
3 potatoes peeled and quartered
1 small onion sliced
1 small can of mushrooms (opt)
3 Tbsp flour
¾ c water

Trim all excess fat from the roast and place in crock pot. Coat meat with the dry onion soup and cream of mushroom soup. Cover and cook on low 7-10 hours. During the last 3-4 hours of cooking time, add the carrots, potatoes, and sliced onion. In the last hour before serving, turn to the high setting. Make a smooth paste with the flour and water and stir into the crock pot to thicken the gravy.

Discussion Questions

1. Claudia discovers that in the right place, at the right time, a person who may seem awkward and gawky to others may be precisely what is needed. Have you seen this truth manifested in your life? Others? Give an example and share.

2. Claudia sees herself from a negative viewpoint and believes she has a black cloud over her head with misfortunes happening when she is around. To fix this, she wants to change herself into something she is not. Pete has a negative view of himself and believes he is unlovable. He compensates by avoidance of relationships. Are these common reactions? Have you experienced these feelings or know of others who have? Share.

3. Pete is an introvert and Claudia an extrovert. Do you believe opposites attract? Could there be a benefit? Why or why not?

4. Claudia thinks she needs to change her black cloud image to find her Prince Charming. But Elaine advises her to fall in love with someone who thinks she's perfect as is. Is this good advice? Are there merits in both viewpoints? Is one viewpoint right or wrong? Explain.

5. Claudia and Elaine made a pact to not speak negatively regarding Claudia's clumsiness. Do you think speaking negatively about yourself makes a difference? Is there value in speaking positively? Share your thoughts.

6. Claudia lost her parents in a boating accident and carries feelings of guilt. Pete harbors hurts from rejection in his past that shape his current fears. Do you have past experiences that have affected who you are today? Did you learn any coping skills? How did you come to grips with those fears? Do you know of others who have had to develop coping skills? Share.

7. In chapter three, Pete wonders if he is witnessing "Kali, the spider, drawing in Claudia, the fly." What is his concern?

8. There are clues that Pete and Claudia are meant for each other. Name some. What do these clues tell someone who is looking for Mr. or Ms. Right?

9. In Chapter six, Claudia believes she ruined Elaine's grand opening by bringing the dogs, who disrupted the ceremony. But she

discovers that the disaster made national news and gave Elaine great publicity. This is an example of good coming from disaster. Romans 8:28 tells us the "all things work together for good to them that love God, to them who are the called according to his purpose" (KJV). Share a circumstance where this truth has been evident in your own life.

10. In chapter seven, Pete's response to Claudia wanting to please Kali by offering an obedience class is harsh. He tells her she shouldn't let people push her around. Francine responds by suggesting prayer. How did Claudia answer each person? How would you have advised Claudia? Is there a place for both types of advice? Explain.

11. Francine witnessed to her husband using bookmarks with Scriptures rather than nagging him. What are other ways to witness about God's goodness without preaching, which sometimes scares people off?

12. Clover seems to be a good judge of character. Have you experienced this with a dog? Share.

13. What do you see as the significance of Kali seeing a four-leaf clover as opposed to Pete seeing a heart in the markings on Clover?

14. Pete and Claudia are able to share with one another in the secret room, yet outside the room communication is thwarted. Why? Are there situations in which you have been able to share your thoughts more freely with others?

15. Pete sees Kali as a threat to Claudia's well-being. Claudia sees her as caring and an encouragement. As the reader, how do you see her?

16. Claudia wants to please. Can that be a good trait? What are the dangers?

17. Claudia's dog theft charge is exposed. Is the reaction of her customers normal? Should we believe all that is in print? Why do people feed on the misfortunes of others?

18. After the fire, Aunt Lucy encourages Claudia to look at the blessings instead of the negatives. Have you experienced a bad situation in which you can see some blessings?

19. Kali has a tendency to use people for her own purposes. Can those traits be turned to positive? How?

20. In chapter 16, Aunt Lucy says, "your past doesn't define you." What does that statement mean to you?

21. Pete believes Claudia has been convinced by Kali to move to Birmingham. Claudia thinks Pete may have told Lyman about the dog theft arrest. Have you ever been mistaken about a situation? How did you learn the truth? How was the misunderstanding rectified?

22. In the end, Francine quotes a saying her husband used to quote, "Those that mind, don't matter and those that matter, don't mind." How did this saying apply in Claudia's situation? Does it apply to anything you or someone close to you has had to deal with?

23. When Pete is leaving to go on the oil rigs, he sees a hermit crab alone in his shell. Is being alone always undesirable? What is the difference between loneliness and solitude?

24. Francine's Scripture bookmarks seem to surface with the right words at the right time. Have you experienced receiving a Scripture just when you needed it? Share.

25. Claudia lays the four-leaf clover necklace given to her by Kali on the altar. What is the significance? What other heavy burdens might be left at the altar?

26. At the end of the story, Richie finds a coin that holds the promise of more adventure. Can you think of a time when you made a special, unexpected discovery? Did it bring change to your life? Explain.

About the Author

Sally Jo Pitts is a writer, private investigator and retired guidance counselor with over twenty years teaching experience in the field of family and consumer sciences. Her passion is investigating, especially when it involves faith-based stories in affairs of the heart. Sally Jo is the author of the romance novel, *And Then Blooms Love*—book #1 of the Hamilton Harbor Legacy series. More about the author and things she investigates can be found at www.sallyjopitts.com.

Made in the USA
Columbia, SC
07 January 2020

86198422R00111